For more than fifty years,
Yearling has been the leading name
in classic and award-winning literature
for young readers.

Yearling books feature children's
favorite authors and characters,
providing dynamic stories of adventure,
humor, history, mystery, and fantasy.

Trust Yearling paperbacks to entertain,
inspire, and promote the love of reading
in all children.

DISCARD

The Flock of Fury

by Thomas E. Sniegoski

illustrated by Eric Powell

A YEARLING BOOK

Published by Yearling, an imprint of Random House Children's Books
a division of Random House, Inc., New York

This is a work of fiction. Names, characters, places, and incidents either are the product
of the author's imagination or are used fictitiously. Any resemblance to actual persons,
living or dead, events, or locales is entirely coincidental.

Text copyright © 2008 by Thomas Sniegoski
Illustrations copyright © 2008 by Eric Powell

Visit us on the Web! www.randomhouse.com/kids

Educators and librarians, for a variety of teaching tools, visit us at
www.randomhouse.com/teachers

Library of Congress Cataloging-in-Publication Data is available upon request.
ISBN: 978-0-440-42237-2 (trade)—ISBN: 978-0-385-90545-9 (lib. bdg.)

Printed in the United States of America

December 2008

10 9 8 7 6 5 4 3 2 1

For Justin, Matthew, Cameron, and Collin,

the newest residents of Monstros City

ACKNOWLEDGMENTS

As with everything that I do, this book would not have been possible without the love and support of my wife, LeeAnne, and Mulder the Wonderdog. I love you both, very much. Special thanks dripping in ectoplasmic goo go out to Stephanie Lane, Christopher Golden, Liesa Abrams, James Mignogna, Dave "Nine Panel Nerds" Kraus, John & Jana, Harry & Hugo, Mike Mignola, Christine Mignola, Katie Mignola, Don Kramer, Greg Skopis, Pete Donaldson, Jon & Flo, Bob & Pat, Kim & Abby, Dan Ouellette, Sheila Walker, Mom & Dad Sniegoski, Mom & Dad Fogg, Eric "Yeah, I know" Powell, and Timothy Cole and the Furious Furies down at Cole's Comics.

Thanks for reading.

CHAPTER 1

Beelzebub Prison:
A very bad place.

The prison guard, who looked like a small Tyrannosaurus rex, attempted to adjust his uniform jacket, but his two tiny front arms couldn't quite get the job done.

"Want me to give you a hand with that, Earl?" the werewolf guard, whose name was Robert, asked his partner.

The two were in the observation tower of the high-security prison, getting ready to begin their outside rounds. It was a quiet night on Scab Island, a small piece of land that squatted like some giant toad in the

Dreadful Ocean, fifty miles from the shores of Monstros City.

"If you wouldn't mind," the dinosaur said, moving closer.

Robert gave the bottom of the dark blue material a good tug, pulling it down over Earl's potbelly. "There," he said, stepping back to admire his work. "How's that?"

"That's great," Earl said, craning his neck to look down. "Probably should think of dropping some weight, y'know? Ever since the wife started taking those Dr. Mellman cooking classes, I've been putting on the poundage."

"Tell me about it," Robert said, opening the door that would take them outside the prison for their nightly ground patrol. "My wife makes these delicious meat sandwiches that she serves in a bowl filled with thick blood gravy."

The two went outside, Earl closing the door behind him with a swipe of his muscular tail.

"Now, do you eat that with your hands or . . ."

"I eat it with a spoon," Robert said, starting across the catwalk that ran along the perimeter of the prison, shining his powerful flashlight out over the shore and onto the water.

"So it's really more like a soup," Earl commented as he followed his partner.

The werewolf stopped and turned to look at his

friend. "No, it's a sandwich. It's made with two slices of bread and has meat in the middle."

"Yeah, but you're eating it with a spoon. . . . Nobody eats a sandwich with a spoon. Sounds more like soup to me . . . or maybe stew."

The werewolf shook his shaggy head. "No, it's not stew and it's not soup, okay? It's a sandwich . . . a sandwich. The only reason I eat it with a spoon is because of all the gravy—it's very messy."

"Is there slurping?" Earl asked very seriously.

"What do you mean is there slurping?"

"When you eat your . . . sandwich with a spoon, is there slurping?"

Robert shrugged. "Maybe a little. There's a lot of blood gravy."

Earl slowly nodded. "I still think it sounds more like a stew than a sandwich."

Robert slapped a clawed hand over his face. "It's not a stew," the werewolf howled, his voice growing louder as he became more frustrated. "It's a sand—"

Just then, something splashed offshore.

"What was that?" Robert asked. He shone the flashlight toward the sound's origin.

"Probably nothing," Earl said. He tried to unhook his own flashlight from his belt, but his arms were too short.

"Gotta hook that closer," he muttered, craning his neck, trying to snag the light with his teeth.

"It's not nothing," Robert said, his beam finding bubbles on the oily surface of the black ocean.

Something big was rising to the surface.

"Wha—what is it?" Earl stammered, drawing closer to his werewolf partner.

Robert shook his shaggy head from side to side as the large, metallic head of a mechanical octopus emerged from the water, followed by multiple tentacles.

"I can't believe it," Robert gasped. "It's a giant robot octopus!"

"Are you sure it's an octopus?" Earl asked, leaning closer to the railing of the platform they were standing on. "Looks more like a giant robot squid to me."

The mechanical octopus—yes, it was an octopus—surged forward in the brackish water with a mighty splash, moving toward the shore and the prison.

"Whatever it is, it's trouble," the werewolf said, reaching for the walkie-talkie at his belt.

But before he could speak, six powerful metal tentacles rocketed up from the water, grabbed hold of the platform and hauled its gigantic body from the water.

The metal walkway squealed like pigs dropped into a wood-chipper as it was twisted, bent and finally ripped from the front of the prison.

Earl and Robert screamed in terror as they fell with the mangled platform to the sandy beach below.

Trapped beneath the wreckage of the platform, all they could do was watch as the giant mechanical octopus crawled up the beach, its metal tentacles reaching to tear down the prison walls.

Mukus cheered wildly as he watched the tentacles of the octocraft tear down Beelzebub's great stone walls.

He and his partner in crime, Klot, stood side by side, peering out the circular window of the octopus-shaped vehicle as the inside of the prison was revealed.

The *Most Dangerous Prisoner Wing,* to be precise.

"I just love it when we get to destroy stuff," Mukus said, barely able to contain his excitement. Rivulets of ooze ran from his face and body, forming thick puddles at his stubby feet.

"Couldn't agree more, my slimy chum," Klot said. He was about to put one of his long, spindly arms around his moist friend's shoulders when he thought better of it.

"And this is just the beginning," a powerful voice behind them boomed.

The two turned to face their villainous master. He sat in a high-backed chair, surrounded by the octocraft's many controls.

The Monarch was a criminal mastermind. Using a series of levers, switches and joysticks, the secret crime lord of Monstros City operated the craft he had designed and built.

"When we are through here, we'll be that much closer to bringing my ingenious plans to fruition," the Monarch announced, his face hidden by the drooping hood of his scarlet robe.

"Can't wait!" Mukus clapped enthusiastically, his gooey bodily fluids splashing his pal.

"Watch it!" Klot said, wiping his red flesh.

Mukus watched as their master reached into his robe and removed a strange handheld device.

"Here is how you will provide me with the ingredients I require to bring about the end of my most hated enemy," the master criminal stated as he passed the device to Mukus.

"Ohhhhhhhh, what is it?" Klot asked, his yellow eyes bulging as he reached to touch it.

"Mine!" Mukus screeched, pulling it away from his companion's spindly fingers.

"No doors will remain locked to you as long as that device is in your possession," the Monarch explained.

"This'll open any door," Mukus whispered excitedly. He'd already started to push the buttons on the front, and the gadget made a noise like a baby chick being squished by a boa constrictor. *Not an unpleasant sound*, the dripping monster thought.

"Go!" the Monarch commanded, and the two lackeys jumped into action.

A door in the front of the octocraft slowly opened, and a tonguelike platform extended down to the prison-wing floor.

"Let me try it," Klot said, again grabbing for the device.

"Watch it with the hands!" Mukus exclaimed, keeping his companion away. "The master gave it to me!"

"But he'd want us to share," Klot said, frustrated. "Why won't you share?"

"Don't you know, silly?" Mukus said with a wet-sounding chuckle. "I'm a bad guy, and bad guys don't share."

They both now stood in the center of a long corridor. Multiple doors faced them—doors that were the only things preventing them from retrieving what their master most desired.

And before Klot could try to take away the electronic key again, Mukus aimed the device at each of the doors in turn and pushed the button repeatedly, making that baby-chick-being-squished sound.

The doors' locking mechanisms slid back, and metallic echoes filled the hall.

"I love that," Mukus said, eyes twinkling with excitement.

"You stink," Klot said, folding his arms across his chest. "Just you wait until the next time I get my hands on a mechanical door-thingy, I'm not gonna let you anywhere near it."

"Don't be such a baby," Mukus muttered, his eyes fixed on the prison-cell doors.

And one by one they slowly opened.

The Bounder boys were the first to emerge, the Slovakian Rot-Toothed Hopping Monkey Demons jumping from their cell and bouncing around Mukus and Klot.

"Ghaaa!" Klot screamed. The five demon monkeys were moving so quickly it was dizzying.

From another cell three more criminals emerged, and Mukus practically squealed with delight.

"Look who it is!" he said excitedly, rivulets of slime dribbling down his body as if from leaky spigots.

"Is—is that the Sassafras Siblings . . . and their mom?" Klot asked, not believing his eyes. The Sassafras Siblings were cooler than a Frost Giant's heart in the criminal community, and their mother . . . a legend.

"It certainly is," Mukus said as the brother and sister trolls escorted their much larger mother out of the prison cell.

From the remaining two cells two more figures emerged, and Mukus thought he just might pass out, he was so star-struck.

"Hold me up, my legs are getting weak," the slimy monster said, falling backward into Klot's arm.

"Are they who I think they are?" Klot asked, holding his friend up.

Mukus nodded ferociously, sending spatters of body slime into the air.

"They are . . . they are," he said. "The Gaseous Ghost and Vomitor."

And all Mukus and Klot could do was stare in awe at the amazing examples of villainy that now stood before them.

They were in the presence of criminal royalty.

"Who are these two?" Mother Sassafras asked with a scowl.

The mother troll was extremely large, her gray prison dress so tight that it looked like it was threatening to burst.

Mukus stepped toward the troll woman, taking her large hand in his.

"We are the monsters that have set you free," he said, planting a particularly drippy kiss on the top of her hand.

"*Yaarrrgh!*" Mother Sassafras bellowed, yanking her hand away. "He's defiled me, children!" she complained, trying to rub off the slime. "Defend your mother's honor and show this dripping ruffian what for."

"He just kissed your hand, Mother," Sigmund said with a roll of his eyes. "I don't think he meant you any harm."

"But what about the germs?" Mother Sassafras asked in a horrified whisper. She looked at her hand as if expecting it to suddenly break out.

"Yes, what about the germs?" Sireena asked, turning toward the dripping beastie and scowling. "How dare you put your filthy lips on my mother's hand?"

Mukus threw up his slimy digits in surrender. "I was only being nice," he apologized. "I meant no insult."

Klot approached to back him up.

"He really didn't," the red-skinned monster explained. "He's always doing stupid stuff like this. He's perfectly harmless."

The released villains glared at them.

"You two are breaking us out?" one of the Bounder boys asked.

"Yes, we are, Benny," Mukus said, reading the name tag on the demon's bright red vest.

"How's that possible?" Bobby Bounder asked. "Look at 'em . . . they're a couple of idiots."

"Hey." Klot spoke up. "If it weren't for us idiots, you'd still be cooling your springy heels behind those locked doors."

"He's got a point, Bobby," Bernie Bounder said.

The other monkey demons all grumbled.

The Gaseous Ghost, his body looking as though it was made from torn rags of smoke, drifted up from the floor, filling the chamber with a horrible stink like rotten eggs. "Be they idiots or geniuses," he said, his voice sounding as though he was speaking underwater, "all that matters is we are free."

"The Ghost is right," Sigmund Sassafras said. "Does it really matter?"

"Can I say something?" Mukus began.

"No!" the short, armored creature called Vomitor barked. When his mouth opened, a loud, liquidy bubbling sound came from within.

"You don't want to get that one angry," Klot told Mukus, subtly making the "puke" gesture while he shook his head.

"Is that a spot?" Mother Sassafras suddenly cried, scrutinizing the back of her hand.

Sireena grabbed it and looked carefully. "Could be," she growled. "It could be the early stages of some foul disease."

She looked up, glaring at Mukus and Klot with

beady, burning eyes. "How dare you give my mother-dearest a disease!"

The large troll had begun to cry, and her son moved to comfort her.

"There, there, Mommy," Sigmund said, taking her hand in his and patting it.

The Bounder boys were growing agitated.

"Look what you did!" Balthasar Bounder screeched. "First you gave her a disease and now she's crying."

Mukus slowly backed up. "I think things are about to get ugly," the slimy monster said to his companion.

"Y'think?" Klot answered, backing into Vomitor who had suddenly appeared behind them, blocking their way.

The Gaseous Ghost floated above the gathering.

"A vote," the ghostly creature stated. "Raise your hand if you wish to utterly destroy these two and then be on our way."

All the villains but Sigmund raised their hands.

For some reason, Mukus found that sort of touching.

"Thanks for your support," he said, nodding in the troll's direction.

Sigmund looked around to see that he was the only one, then quickly raised his hand.

"Nice," Mukus said angrily.

"It's decided then," the Ghost said.

With murder in their eyes, they all began to converge on Mukus and Klot.

But before they could reach them, the chamber was suddenly filled with a blinding light.

"What transpires here?" asked a voice dripping with authority and menace.

As the villains shielded their eyes from the light, Mukus and Klot turned to see their master.

"My eyes!" Mother Sassafras bellowed. "I think my corneas might be damaged!"

The light from the octocraft dimmed, revealing the impressive form of the Monarch standing in the doorway.

"Thanks, boss," Mukus said as he and Klot scurried up the platform to hide behind their master's robe. "I think things were about to get out of hand."

"First Mother's given a disease, and now her corneas are singed," Sireena Sassafras said. "I'd say this calls for murder."

The other villains agreed and they made their move toward the scarlet-robed figure.

But the Monarch just raised one of his gloved hands, revealing a strange device hidden in the palm of his hand.

"Come no further," he ordered as the device began

to glow. "I am the Monarch and you will know the power of my criminal genius."

Klot and Mukus gasped as the evildoers were suddenly engulfed in an odd yellow light and began to float off the floor, hovering in the air. Slowly they drifted back toward their still-open prison cells.

"Wait . . . what are you doing?" Sireena Sassafras cried out, her thick legs pedaling the air.

"I'm putting you back," the Monarch proclaimed. "It would appear I was mistaken about your desire to be free."

"*No!*" the former prisoners, who were about to be prisoners again, bellowed in unison.

"No?" the Monarch repeated. "Then why were you about to harm my trusted lackeys?" He gestured to Mukus and Klot, still standing behind him.

"It was a mistake!" Bailey Bounder yelled.

"A mistake?" the Monarch questioned, stroking his chin, hidden within the darkness of his hood. "How interesting."

He pointed the glowing device at them, slowly drawing them back.

"Then am I to believe that you would be willing to serve my every command in exchange for your freedom?"

"Yes!" they all answered together.

"You will listen to my every instruction and carry them out to the last detail without question?"

"Yes!" they answered again.

"And the hate I have for my most reviled enemy shall become your hate as well?" the Monarch asked.

"Yes!" they shouted, but it was Sireena whose curiosity got the better of her.

"Not to be rude, but who exactly do you want us to hate so much?" she asked, still floating above the prison floor.

The Monarch remained silent, but Mukus could see the telltale tightening of his master's fists.

"The hero of Monstros City—Owlboy," the Monarch proclaimed, his voice trembling with suppressed rage. "You will help me destroy him."

The criminals slowly nodded in agreement.

"Owlboy, eh?" Sireena said with a laugh as she was lowered to the ground with the others.

All the villains were smiling now.

"Hating him as much as you do is gonna be easy," she said, rubbing her clawed hands together.

CHAPTER 2

Billy still hadn't decided what to do for his science fair project.

As he made his way into Mr. Harpin's class, his brain was on fire with all the possibilities.

Back home in his workshop, he had a corner set aside for just such projects. The homemade laser gun was cool, as was a project on the solar system and the one about turning potatoes into batteries, but he thought the volcano was probably the best of the bunch.

Billy smiled as he took his seat. He would build a working miniature of Mount Vesuvius, which erupted on August 24 in A.D. 79, burying the city of Pompeii and everybody who lived there beneath ash and lava.

Wicked cool!

He glanced around the room, watching as his pals took their seats. He wondered what their projects would be.

Danny Ashwell was the champ of science fairs, always managing to come up with stuff both disgusting and fascinating. Billy remembered his friend's groundbreaking presentation last year, "Fun with Fungus." It was awesome. Fungi were Danny's forte, and they all bowed before his mastery.

Billy could hear Dwight boasting about his project from the back of the class, and he chuckled to himself. He figured Dwight would probably do that whole fossil thing again. Dwight had gone out west one summer and brought back supposedly genuine fossilized dinosaur bones.

Billy always thought that they looked like dirty chicken bones, but he didn't have the heart to shatter poor Dwight's dreams.

Reggie was sitting quietly at his desk, going through books one after another. He was scrambling to find something fast and easy. Billy made a mental note to help his buddy out with one of his own projects if Reggie needed it.

Kathy B waved to catch Billy's eye, and he waved back. He wondered what the drama queen was going to do. As far as he knew, Shakespeare hadn't been much of a scientist, but then again, Billy didn't really know all that much about the guy. For all he knew, Shakespeare could have invented a way to generate power using boring plays.

The classroom sounded like feeding time at the monkey house until Mr. Harpin came in. The science teacher, an older man who wore his pants a little too high, put his plastic briefcase on the desk and motioned for the class to settle down.

He snapped open the case, removed his attendance sheet and shuffled through his notes. Then he removed a pair of thick, horn-rimmed glasses from his shirt pocket, put them on and cleared his throat.

"Today you were to surprise me with the wondrous and exciting topics you have chosen for your science fair projects," Mr. Harpin said, his voice, as usual, void of any emotion. If it was one day revealed that his science teacher was in fact a killer robot from the future, Billy would have very little problem believing it.

"And I was going to surprise you by announcing that all of my classes have been registered to participate in the *Science Is Awesome* statewide competition that I believed would take place four months from now."

Mr. Harpin paused, looking around the room with his flat, mechanical gaze.

"My belief, however, was incorrect," he continued.

"The date of the competition was changed, and unfortunately, I did not receive the updated information until this morning. The competition is now only two weeks away."

Billy felt a pang of disappointment. It would have been totally cool to bring his Vesuvius model to the *Science Is Awesome* event, but they'd never be able to participate now if it was only two weeks away.

"So, in order for this to work, I have devised a way in which we should still be able to participate. The science projects will be different this year."

Billy's ears immediately perked up. *Different? How different? I don't like different. Different is too . . . different!* his brain chattered.

"This year, your science projects will be done in teams," Mr. Harpin said. Billy felt the floor beneath his feet begin to crumble.

That certainly is different.

"Not only do I believe that this will allow the projects to be done in time for the statewide competition, but it will also be an important exercise in promoting teamwork," the science teacher explained.

Billy felt himself begin to sweat, his skin tingling and itching as if ants—a *colony* of ants—were crawling beneath his clothes. Just the thought of others claiming the rights to his Vesuvius project was enough to get him all worked up.

He tried to think of something good that might come from this, deciding that if he could pick his own team, maybe . . .

"I have already assigned teams and you will find them posted on the wall outside after class," Mr. Harpin went on, destroying just about any chance of a silver lining.

And to make it worse, Billy then had to wait, sitting through a lecture on the incredibly short lifespan of the common fruit fly.

Billy never would have imagined he could be jealous of a fruit fly.

After class that day, Billy found himself holding back from the list, like a prisoner sentenced to hang making his way slowly to the gallows.

His friends were huddled around the list with the rest of his classmates.

Danny was the first to look away from the list, his face as white as a sheet.

"Is it that bad?" Billy asked in a shaky whisper.

"For me, not so much," Danny said. "But for you . . ."

Kathy B, Dwight and Reggie had made it to the front of the group.

"O thou monster Ignorance," Kathy B cried. "How deformed dost thou look!"

Billy had no idea what Shakespeare play that line was from, or even what it really meant, but he was smart enough to know that it couldn't be anything good. He began to push his way through the diminishing crowd, making brief eye contact with Reggie.

"I'm sorry, Billy," he said with a loud slurp, wiping the drool from his braces with the sleeve of his shirt.

"Dude," Dwight said, shaking his head behind Reggie. "I'll tell your mother that you loved her or something."

Billy was confused. "I don't get it."

"After you see your team you will," Dwight said, moving away.

Joshua Stepenmyer and Stephanie Demascus stepped back, allowing Billy to scoot in and finally read the list.

How bad could it be?

His eyes traveled down the list. He found his name and the others that would make up his team.

Billy started to scream, not sure he would ever be able to stop.

"Is there a problem, Mr. Hooten?" an authoritative voice asked.

"Why?" Billy shrieked, turning to face Mr. Harpin while pointing a trembling finger back toward the list.

"Why what, Mr. Hooten?"

"Why . . . *them?*" he managed to spit out.

Mr. Harpin put on his glasses and started to read.

"Oh yes, your team," he said.

The science teacher removed the glasses and slipped them back into his shirt pocket. "I see this as a perfect opportunity for you to practice your leadership skills."

"Leadership skills?" Billy screamed. "Who said anything about me wanting to be a leader? I'd have better luck leading a pack of wild monkeys."

A sudden hush came over the hallway and Billy realized that everyone was staring at something down the hall.

He just about threw up his pounding heart when he saw Randy Kulkowski, Mitchell Spivey, Darious "insane in the membrane" Fontague and Penny "one brow" Feryurthotuss, all standing there.

His team.

Waiting for him.

"Hey, Hooten," Randy called out as he strolled down the hall, the others following closely, looking amused. "Are you as excited as we are to all be on the same team?"

"I'm totally thrilled," Billy said, his voice lacking all emotion.

Mr. Harpin patted Billy on the back. "Attaboy," the

old science teacher said. "That's exactly the kind of team spirit I'm looking for."

Randy's smile grew wide, revealing yellow teeth flecked with pieces of meals past. "With you on our team we're probably gonna have the best project in the whole state!"

"Yeah, best in the whole state," Mitchell repeated, and started to laugh.

Darious stepped forward to look at Billy with crazy eyes. "I remember you." He pointed at Billy's chest. "You took my Jell-O in first grade."

Billy shook his head. "I didn't even know you in first grade. It must've been somebody else."

"Maybe," Darious said, stroking his chin. "I still miss that Jell-O."

Penny snapped her gum bullwhip-loud and looked at her long, curved fingernails. They were painted a disgusting shade of baby-poop green.

"I hate science," she stated.

"And that's why it's so freakin' awesome that we got Hooten here to help us," Randy said. He threw an arm around Billy's shoulders and gave him a hug that nearly squeezed every bit of air from his lungs.

"This is gonna be awesome."

Mr. Harpin cleared his throat to get everybody's attention. "Tomorrow's science class will meet in the auditorium. You will have an opportunity to meet with your teams, choose your topics and assign responsibilities to each team member."

Randy gave Billy a punch in the arm that caused his entire skeletal structure to vibrate painfully.

"That oughta be good," Randy said. "We'll figure out who's doing what."

Billy didn't need the meeting in the auditorium to tell him:

He would be doing it all.

CHAPTER 3

Billy spent the rest of the day in a kind of shock, seeing Randy, Mitchell and the other members of his science project team smiling at him around every corner.

By the time the last bell of the day had rung, and he found himself outside in the cool winter air, he was a nervous wreck.

"How y'doin', Billy?"

He turned to see Reggie and the gang heading toward him.

Billy just shrugged, completely in a funk.

"Hey, Bill, I've been thinking," Dwight said. "Have you ever thought of leaving the country . . . maybe hopping a train to Russia or something?"

Billy glared at his supposed friend.

"How about a head injury?" Kathy B suggested. "Something that requires extensive hospitalization might do the trick." Her eyes twinkled with the brilliance of her idea. "That way you won't have to participate because you'll be recuperating."

"Thanks, but no thanks, guys," Billy said. "I'm gonna have to figure out how to get out of this one on my own."

Danny came up alongside him and threw a chubby arm around his shoulder. "I know exactly how you're feeling, Billy."

"You do?"

The boy nodded. "I'm not sure how my own genius is going to mix with the mundane intelligence of my team. Will they even understand the complexities of fungus growth? Something tells me that's a big no."

"Yeah," Billy said, removing Danny's arm. "Your situation is just like mine."

He decided that he'd had enough help from his friends and gave them a halfhearted wave as he left them.

"See ya tomorrow, Billy!" Reggie cried. "Unless you've gone to Russia or banged up your head!"

Billy didn't even bother to turn around, continuing down the street from Connery Elementary toward downtown Bradbury.

He was feeling so low that he was desperate to feel

anything other than horrible, and this being new comic book day, he could think of no better place than the Hero's Hovel to maybe restore a little bit of sunshine to his bleak and gloomy mood.

The bell over the store's door rang cheerily. Billy resisted the urge to jump up, rip the bell from the doorframe and throw it across the room.

Claudius, the store owner's German shepherd, got up from his place on the floor near the cash register and woofed happily, then trotted over to give Billy a sniff.

"Hey, kid," Cole said, coming out of the back room drinking from a tall bottle of Zap cola. "What's cookin'?"

Billy grunted, going right to the new comic book section.

The week's selections were pretty awesome, but just when he would feel himself getting excited, he would remember what awaited him in school the next day. He thought he just might throw up on the new arrivals.

"Anything catch your eye?" Cole asked, coming around the rack.

"Nah," Billy said crankily. "Kind of a crappy week."

Cole was now standing beside him. Not even the store owner's insanely bright Hawaiian shirt was cheering him up.

"Sounds like you might need one of these," Cole said, handing Billy an already-opened bottle of Zap.

Billy took the bottle with a sad *thanks* and drank a small sip.

"When somebody as crazy about superheroes as you isn't excited about the first issue of *Ultimate Disaster on Multiple Worlds in Crisis*, I know something must be up."

They sat down in the back room of the Hovel to talk. Billy ended up spilling his guts to Cole about the situation at school.

"Hmmm, that's bad," Cole agreed, taking a long pull from his bottle of cola.

"Don't I know it," Billy agreed.

"Short of running off to Russia or getting some kind of debilitating head trauma that puts you in the hospital, I can't think of any way you can avoid it."

Billy took a long drink from his own bottle to drown his sorrows.

"You're gonna hate to hear this, but I think the only thing you can do is suck it up and make the best of it."

"Make the best of it?" Billy asked with a scowl. "There's no best about it. . . . These guys are animals and they're gonna make my life a complete nightmare. I'll be doing all the work!"

"I know it's tough, kid, but sometimes that's just how it is," Cole said.

Billy expected at least a little bit of sympathy from Cole, but then he figured maybe Cole just didn't remember how tough things could be when you were twelve.

"I had the coolest science project planned," Billy said, getting up from his seat to take the Zap bottle over to the wooden case where the empties were stored. "And now I'm going to have to share it with a buncha Neanderthals."

Cole chuckled and Billy turned to glare at him.

"It's not funny at all."

"Sorry, Bill. I know it's not funny, and I also know exactly how you feel."

Billy returned to his chair, plopping down as if his depression had turned his bones to rubber.

"How can you possibly know how I feel?"

"It was a long time ago, when I was first starting out in the comic book biz," the store owner began to explain. Cole had once been a comic book artist.

"My publisher had given me an assignment drawing an issue of *Cutie Pie Comics*."

"*Cutie Pie Comics*?" Billy questioned, wrinkling his nose with distaste.

"Yeah, I felt the same way," Cole said. "I wasn't into funny animal books, but I needed the work, so I couldn't turn it down."

"What did you do?" Billy asked, curious as to where this story was going.

"Everything but," Cole said. "I didn't want anything to do with *Cutie Pie Comics*, so I did everything I could not to work on it, but the deadline came closer and closer."

"Did you finally end up doing it?"

Cole nodded. "Eventually I just realized that it wasn't going to go away, so I sucked it up and started drawing. I made it easier on myself by trying to find one thing . . . just one thing that I enjoyed about drawing Cutie Pie and his friends. See what I'm getting at?"

Billy did see, but as hard as he tried, he couldn't find a single thing about his current situation that wasn't absolutely horrifying.

The Monarch stepped from behind the curtain of his secret laboratory into complete and utter chaos.

The villains he had recently released were in the meeting room, arguing and carrying on like a bunch of six-year-old pageant contestants at the Little Miss Darling competition.

Sigmund Sassafras was in the middle of a chest-thumping competition with Bernie Bounder, while the other four Bounder boys looked on. The Gaseous Ghost was flying around Mother Sassafras's head while she tried to swat him from the sky for ruining her hairdo, and Sireena Sassafras was threatening Vomitor for getting some of his toxic spew on her shoe.

The Monarch thought his head might explode from all the ruckus.

He saw that Mukus and Klot had retreated to the far corner of the room, unable to control the gathering of villainy.

The king of crime in Monstros loudly cleared his throat.

The villains halted their business only momentarily, looking in his direction before continuing with their clamor.

The Monarch began to fume.

"Silence!" he commanded, raising one of his gloved hands above his hooded head to emphasize his authority. The villains stopped. He could tell that they were not happy about it, but at least they were quiet.

"Do not make me regret freeing you from your cells at Beelzebub," the Monarch warned.

Now that there was silence in the room, his lackeys made their way toward where he stood, just in case he should need something from them. He had trained the two monsters well.

"We all share a common hate," he said, addressing his villainous audience.

In the room's center was a small round table with chairs around it, and one by one the villains took a seat.

"I hate him," Mother Sassafras said, pointing to the Gaseous Ghost, who did not sit in a seat but floated above it.

"And I hate you," the Ghost responded, his smoky body changing color with this declaration.

"I'm not fond of any of you, really," Sireena said, pulling a small mirror from her handbag and checking her makeup.

Vomitor rolled his large, circular eyes.

"Wait a minute," Sigmund said, getting up from his chair. "Can't we just behave ourselves for a little while . . . to hear what the Monarch has to say? It's the least we can do for the one who set us free."

The villains grumbled.

"When did you get so rational?" Sireena snarled.

"I'll show you rational," Sigmund growled, raising his fist to his sister.

"Children, children, you play nice, now," Mother Sassafras warned. "Or I'll rip both your heads off and use them for bowling."

"I hate bowling," Vomitor bellowed, his tiny fist clenched in rage.

The Bounder boys began to bounce higher and higher.

Suddenly, an earsplitting shriek filled the air and the villains grabbed their heads in agony.

The Monarch held a small microphone-shaped device above his head.

"Are we ready to behave?" the king of villains asked.

They calmed down and he turned off the wailing device.

"Very good," the Monarch said, peering out at them from within the darkness of his hood. "I want you all to use that hate seething inside you on the correct enemy."

An eye-shaped television monitor dropped down from the ceiling with a hum.

"Are we going to watch a movie?" Bobby Bounder asked his brothers. "I hope it's *Jurassic Pork*. I love movies about giant killer pigs."

Mukus cleared his throat. "We're not showing *Jurassic Pork*," he announced, then turned to his master. "Right?"

"Correct," the Monarch said.

Scenes of the busy streets of Monstros appeared on the screen—all manner of ghoulie, ghostie and long-legged beastie moving about the sprawling city.

"I thought we were going to see what we should be using our hate on," Sireena said, watching the city scenes with an ugly scowl.

The Monarch pointed to the screen.

"That is your target," he proclaimed.

The villains stared, their mouths hanging open stupidly.

"I don't get it," Vomitor announced with a low and rumbling voice.

The Monarch stepped in front of the eye-shaped monitor.

"I want you to pounce on the city. Let them know that you are no longer locked away behind the bars of Beelzebub Prison. Total chaos is your game."

The villains were silent, some attempting to see the screen around the shape of the Monarch.

"But if we do that, wouldn't it alert Owlboy?" the Gaseous Ghost asked.

The Monarch nodded.

"Exactly, and then he'll be right where we want him."

The villains thought about that for a moment, and most nodded in understanding.

The Monarch was starting to get through to them.

"I thought we were going to watch *Jurassic Pork*," Mother Sassafras suddenly said.

Well, some of them, anyway.

Billy's mother called that night's supper "surprise, surprise," because she couldn't ever remember what ingredients went into it. She knew most of the vegetables, but couldn't remember what kind of meat. It could have been mastodon, for all she knew.

Billy sometimes worried that his own memory might get bad, but then other things in his rather complicated life would come along, and he figured that a poor memory would be the least of his problems.

The hot meal could have tasted great . . . or not, but Billy didn't know, because even his taste buds were distracted by his predicament at school.

"Everything all right, pal?" his mother asked in between mouthfuls.

He'd probably taken two or three bites of his supper before his mind drifted off, the grotesque faces of his science project team floating before his eyes.

"Sure," he grumbled. "Everything's just awesome."

"Troubles at school?" she asked. "Anything I can help you with?"

He dropped his fork and started to talk, all his pent-up frustration spilling out of him in one steady stream as he explained what had happened that day in science class.

Running out of air, he barely managed to finish off his last sentence with a squeaking final two words. He gasped for breath and slumped back in his chair.

He expected his mother to sympathize. Which meant he was shocked by the sudden smile that appeared on her face.

"I think that sounds fabulous," she said, reaching for a slice of bread from the basket in the center of the table. "A chance to make some new friends, to get out of that room of yours and away from those musty old funny books." She took a hunk of butter and spread it on the bread. "I think it'll be good for you."

Billy was speechless.

His own mother—siding with Mr. Harpin, throwing him to the hungry wolves.

"Sounds like it stinks to me," Dad said, shoveling another forkful of "surprise, surprise" into his mouth.

He hadn't even looked up from his mysterious supper.

"You do?" Billy asked.

Dad nodded. "It's tough to work with a team that you like, never mind a bunch of blockheads. If man was supposed to work in teams, we all would've been born triplets."

And after those words, his father continued to eat his meal in silence.

Billy couldn't have agreed more.

There was no more talk about it as they finished supper and brought the plates to the counter to be scraped clean and washed.

Billy dried while his mother washed. Dad retreated to the living room, the evening news blaring in the background.

Finishing the last plate, Billy placed it in the cabinet and hung the dish towel over the handle on the front of the oven.

"Going to do my homework," he said, heading out of the kitchen to go upstairs.

"Hey, Billy?" his mother called to him.

He stopped in the hallway, turning to face her.

"Yeah, Mom?"

"Give it a chance," she said with a smile. "Who knows, maybe you'll have a good time."

He knew she meant well, but she just didn't understand the reality of the situation. Billy gave her a smile that said he would try, but deep down he knew that wouldn't be the case at all.

Climbing the stairs, he planned the remainder of the night. He wanted to do his homework and then make a quick trip to Monstros for some Owlboy action.

Just thinking of the city of monsters, and what he might be called upon to do there as their one and only superhero, was enough to lift his spirits.

All day he had denied himself the pleasure of thinking about Monstros, believing that the badness of the day could somehow taint the only cool thing he still had some measure of control over in his life.

Billy couldn't wait to put on his Owlboy costume and get to Monstros.

But first there was geometry to do.

CHAPTER 4

Billy didn't think he'd ever finish his homework.

First there was the geometry assignment, followed by some reading for English class, and then some more reading for world history. He thought his eyes might just melt into his head. Only the thought of going to Monstros for some Owlboy adventuring kept him going until finally he wrapped up his schoolwork for the night.

He grabbed his book bag, with his Owlboy costume stuffed inside, and sneaked down to the kitchen as his parents dozed in front of the TV. It was freakin' cold out, so he made sure to put on his heavy winter coat before heading outside, over the stone wall and into the Pine Hill Cemetery, which bordered his backyard.

He didn't even care about how chilly it was as he entered the Sprylock family mausoleum and changed from his street clothes into his superhero costume; just thinking about the adventure that awaited him was enough to keep him warm.

Dressed as Owlboy, he pushed back the lid on the stone crypt and descended the set of stairs within, being extra careful not to trip on his way down. All he needed was a broken skull to add to his troubles.

No, thank you.

Over the last few months, it had become easier for him to navigate the shadowy passages that could take him to various places in Monstros, as well as to Owlboy's supersecret headquarters, the Roost, which was exactly where he was going.

" 'Sup, homeys!" Billy yelled excitedly as he burst through the door into the monitoring station of the Roost.

Halifax—a troll and phenomenal fix-it guy—and Archebold—a tuxedo-wearing goblin who was Owlboy's sidekick and teacher about all things Monstros—were sitting in some comfy chairs in front of multiple stacked television sets tuned to various locations around the city of monsters. Both were reading magazines and snacking on treats that, up until a few months ago, would have totally disgusted Billy.

"Homeys?" Archebold guestioned, looking up from his magazine.

Billy adjusted his goggles and shrugged. "Heard some kids at school say it and I thought it sounded cool." He moved over between them. "So, what's going on?"

Halifax took a fried bat wing from a bag and munched on it. "Nothing," he said, licking his fingers clean of bat grease.

"Just catching up on some reading," Archebold agreed.

There was a sudden flash of flame and Billy leapt into action.

"Get back!" he screeched. "I think we're under attack."

"No, we're not," Halifax said. "It's just those two goofing around." He nodded toward the corner of the room.

There was another flash of flame, and this time Billy saw the culprits.

Ferdinand, the little dragon, and an equally small Zis-Boom-Bah were chasing each other around.

Billy smiled as he watched the two beasties play. It made him happy to see that the once-hundred-foot-tall monster named Zis-Boom-Bah, who had terrified Monstros not all that long ago, seemed to be adjusting to his new size without any problem, and had found a playmate in the red-skinned minidragon. The decision to leave him this size after using Dr. Bug's shrink gun on him seemed to have been the right one.

"They're having a good time," Billy said as Zis-Boom-Bah grabbed Ferdinand's tail with his gorilla-like hands. The dragon screeched, spinning around and blasting her playmate's feet with a plume of fire.

"Yep," Archebold said, licking a stubby finger and turning the page of his magazine. "Most action we've seen tonight."

Billy sighed as he pulled up a chair to sit down with his friends.

"You mean there's nothing going on?" he asked, already feeling his thoughts start to wander in the direction of his science fair problems.

"Nope," Archebold said. "It's been completely dead since—"

Hoot! Hoot! Hoot! Hoot! Hoot! An alarm sounded.

"What the . . . ?" Archebold said, climbing from his chair to look at the screens. "Oh jeez." Reams of information spilled from the printer. "Looks like I spoke too soon," the goblin said, reading through the printouts.

"What's going on?" Halifax asked, pouring the remains of his fried bat wings into his mouth, crumbs sticking attractively to his furry face.

"You name it," Archebold said, reading one report after another. "It's total chaos out there."

Billy made a move toward the hallway that would take him to the garage and the many Owl-vehicles at their disposal. "Then there isn't a moment to lose!" he announced. "We'll handle things one threat at a time."

Archebold let the papers drop to the floor. "That isn't going to be fast enough."

"It's gonna have to be," Billy said. "I can't be in more than one place at a time, y'know."

Archebold didn't move; he just stood there as Halifax watched.

"There is another way," the goblin said thoughtfully.

"You don't mean . . . ?" Halifax began.

The goblin nodded.

"What the heck are you two doing?" Billy yelled. "There are monsters out there that need our help and you two are just standing around?"

"Should we show him what we've been working on?" Archebold asked the troll.

Halifax agreed and the two creatures suddenly bolted from the room.

"Where are you going?" Billy hollered, the hooting alarm still blaring in the confines of the monitoring room. He was thinking he might have to go out there and try to handle things all by himself when the pair suddenly returned.

"Well, what do you think?" Archebold asked,

showing off the new costume he was wearing. Halifax was wearing one as well and seemed equally proud.

Their costumes were like Billy's Owlboy costume, with little changes here and there.

"Why are you dressed like me?" Billy asked.

"Well, Halifax and I got to thinking the other day—"

"Dangerous," Billy interrupted. "Very dangerous."

"Whatever," Archebold said, going on. "We were thinking about situations very much like this one and decided that you could use some real superhero side-kicks to help when things get out of hand."

"Sidekicks?" Billy asked, not at all sure about what he was hearing.

"I'm OwlLad," Archebold said proudly.

"And I'm the Hooter!" Halifax said, sticking out his prominent potbelly.

"I—I don't know what to say," Billy stammered.

"There's nothing to say," Archebold said. "Monstros needs Owlboy to save the day, and if they can't have that, sidekicks are the next best thing."

Halifax—or the Hooter—reached into the over-stuffed pouches of his utility belt and removed three devices.

"These are communicators, so we can stay in touch," the troll said, handing one to Billy, the other to

Archebold. "We'll keep them on at all times just to let each other know how we're making out."

"Who's going to watch the monitors?" Billy asked, almost convinced.

Archebold pointed to Ferdinand and Zis-Boom-Bah.

"You two hold down the fort," the goblin ordered before dashing toward the elevator.

"Them?" Billy asked as Halifax pulled him from the room.

But there really wasn't any choice. Things were moving way too fast, but it didn't change the fact that the city needed Owlboy.

The city needed *them*.

If Billy had been looking for something to get his mind off his troubles, the roaring Owlpack was it. It was just too bad that it had taken multiple threats on the city of monsters to finally distract him.

The rocket pack strapped to his back—one of Halifax's inventions, which had recently gone through some upgrades (the old one was prone to explode once it got overheated)—propelled Owlboy through the velvet black sky, on his way to a confrontation with one of the threats that had recently emerged.

He was headed toward the Monstros City Mall, the largest shopping establishment in the city of monsters. If there was any place that evil could strike and do a ton of damage, it was the mall.

Billy heard a small pinging sound from the onboard controls of the rocket pack, telling him that he was nearing his destination. He adjusted his goggles and peered down at the mammoth structure. He was amused to see that the mall was shaped like a giant spider.

How freakin' cool is that?

Using a hand control to steer, Billy angled the rocket pack to take him to the parking lot in front of the sprawling shopping complex. He needed to get the lay of the land before charging into battle.

Billy touched down between a full row of parked vehicles, his rocket jets shutting down with a loud *whoosh* as he felt the ground beneath his rubber boots.

Strange, monstrous faces peered out at him from behind the cars and trucks as he unbuckled himself from his bright yellow flying apparatus.

"Hello?" he called. "It's all right to come out, I'm here to help."

Slowly the patrons of the mall began to emerge, recognizing him for who he was.

"You're Owlboy," a squat creature wrapped entirely

in filthy bandages said as he stepped out from behind a brightly colored van. "I was wondering if we'd see you. . . . It's terrible . . . terrible, I say!"

"What's going on?" Billy asked, looking toward the mall entrance.

A giant earthworm wearing a hockey helmet slithered out from beneath a car.

"I was just making a quick stop for some hand cream—"

"Hand cream?" Billy asked, not seeing any hands on the big worm.

"Is there a problem?" the worm asked.

"No, go on," Billy urged.

"I was going in for some hand cream when everything just went crazy. People started screaming when the smashing began."

"What was doing the smashing?" Billy asked, formulating his battle plan. He thought that a call to Archebold might be in order. Hopefully the little goblin had taken the *Book of Creeps* with him on his own mission.

"I don't know," the worm said, obviously still shaken. "Whatever it was, it was moving too fast for me to see."

"And then there was the shooting," the bandaged beastie added. "Don't forget about the shooting."

"Did you see who was doing that?" Billy probed.

"Trolls," a giant spider said, his spindly body slowly coming down from a strand of webbing attached to one of the parking lot lights. "A family of trolls. I could tell they were a family because the boy and girl troll were calling the bigger one Mommy."

"So let me get this straight," Billy said. "We've got something moving so fast that it can't be seen and a family of trolls shooting weapons. Is that it?"

"And they were all out of the Dr. Mellman's Home Surgery Kits," said an ugly little creature clutching an enormous handbag and wearing a flowered housecoat. It had scurried out from its hiding place to be heard.

"That's not a crime," Billy said with a shake of his head.

"It is if you really wanted one," the ugly little creature said haughtily.

Billy turned toward the mall entrance, psyching himself up to enter.

"They attacked the snack shop first," the bandaged creature said, its voice trembling with emotion. "What kind of person goes after poor defenseless snacks, I ask you?"

In Monstros it was all about the snacks, and Billy could feel the citizens' pain.

"Don't you worry," he reassured the crowd. "Owlboy will take care of this."

Puffing out his chest, he strode toward the entrance.

The doors opened on their own when he stepped on the rubber mats just outside.

He paused momentarily and turned back to the parking lot. A few in the crowd gave him the thumbs-up, and he returned the gesture before entering the mall.

Just inside the door Billy stopped to observe his surroundings. There were stores as far as the eye could see, and some evidence of violence: broken glass lay everywhere, and some of the window displays were all messed up.

The snack store was just ahead, and he could see that it had been hit the hardest. Whoever—whatever—had attacked the store had a real sweet tooth: there were candy wrappers scattered all over the floor, both inside and outside the store.

Billy bent down to pick up one of the wrappers, and the smell wafted up into his nostrils.

Grape bubble gum.

Alarms went off in his head, but before he could process the information, things suddenly went crazy.

Shapes moving incredibly fast—bouncing like Super Balls on an overdose of Zap cola—were flying all around him, going so fast that he could barely make them out. He guessed that there were four—no, five of them, and he watched as they ricocheted off the walls, crashing through the windows of the snack store before bouncing outside again to do more damage elsewhere.

Attempting to keep his eyes on at least one of the

furiously bouncing shapes, he tried to figure out what it was he was looking at.

That alarm inside his head was still ringing like crazy.

Grape bubble gum, bouncing: there's something to this, Billy thought.

He played with the switches on his goggles, wondering if there were any special features that would allow him to see exactly what the shapes were. Keeping the bouncing forms in his line of sight, he pushed a button that he'd never really played with before. The bounding shape suddenly froze; and right then he knew why the clues seemed so familiar.

It was the Bounder boys—Slovakian Rot-Toothed Hopping Monkey Demons on a rampage.

But aren't they in jail?

He didn't have time to worry about that; they were here at the moment, making a mess of everything. Owlboy had to stop them, no matter what.

"Hey, Bounder boys!" he yelled, running to the center of the mall trying to get their attention.

One of the monkey demons stopped bouncing long enough to snarl at him through crooked yellow teeth. Billy could read the name tag on his red vest: BOBBY BOUNDER.

"We were wondering how long it would take for you to notice it was us," the monkey demon snarled. "Do you like our new shoes?" he asked, pointing to his clunky footwear with its huge black springs.

That explained how they were bouncing around so quickly. Billy didn't remember their being able to bounce quite this fast the last time he'd encountered them.

"Nice," Billy said.

He heard the twang of coiled springs behind him and turned to see the other Bounder boys—Benny, Bernie, Balthasar and Bailey—all settling down long enough to be seen and encircling him.

"No glue on the floor to help you now, Owlboy," Balthasar spat excitedly.

"And even if there were, we wouldn't be so stupid as to fall for that trap a second time," Benny stated.

"Fool me once, shame on me, fool me twice . . . and a bear poops in the woods," Bailey Bounder taunted.

"Ew!" Billy said, wrinkling his nose.

"What are you talking about?" Benny asked.

"It's an old saying," Bailey answered. "Don't tell me you've never heard it."

"I've never heard such a thing," Balthasar stated. "I think you probably got it wrong."

"Are you telling me I'm stupid?" Bailey screeched, slowly bouncing on the coils of his shoes.

"Guys! Guys!" Bobby called. "A little focus here, please!"

The Bounders were completely wrapped up in their argument, and Billy realized that this would be a perfect time for him to strike. Feeling around one of the pouches on his belt, he tried to remember what kind of weapons he had brought with him. He knew he had smoke bombs, but he wasn't sure they would do the trick.

I need something to slow them down, Billy thought, going through the objects in one pouch, then another. Most of what he found was pretty useless, aside from the smoke bombs: some string, an old AAA battery and a raisin that looked like the Frankenstein monster if he held it at just the right angle.

He was about to give the smoke bombs a try by throwing them down and using the choking cover to knock the Bounders out before they could start bouncing again, but then the explosions started.

The Slovakian Rot-Toothed Hopping Monkey Demons seemed to be as surprised as he was when the sudden detonation tossed them all into the air.

For a moment, as he picked himself up unsteadily from the ground, he almost believed that the cavalry had arrived, that the Monstros City police force had come to give him a hand with the monkey demons.

But then he saw the shapes as they emerged from the dust and smoke, and he knew that these three were about as far from the cavalry as you could get.

The Sassafras Siblings and another, even larger troll that could very well be . . . their mother?

"Do you see what happens when we have to wait for you?" Sireena Sassafras screeched, loading another explosive round into her gigantic rifle. "The stinking monkeys almost got him before us!"

"Can I help it if I had to go to the bathroom?" the giant troll answered furiously. "When nature calls, a woman must answer."

"Leave Mother alone," Sigmund warned his sister. "You know she has an incredibly small bladder for a troll her size."

Billy was right; the siblings did have their mother along for their latest round of destruction. As he ran for cover, he wondered why they weren't in jail.

"There he goes!" Sireena cried, aiming her weapon and firing.

Billy dove below a squirting fountain just as it exploded into smithereens. Brushing dirt and dust off his costume, he started running again as missile-like projectiles decimated the mall around him.

This is wicked bad, he thought, turning around briefly.

The scene was worse than he imagined.

The Bounders and the Sassafrases had joined together and were coming his way.

Mother Sassafras, as if wanting to make up for being

54

late, pushed her way ahead of her children excitedly. "I've been waiting to do this for a long time," she bellowed, two huge pistols clutched in her chubby hands.

Billy dove just as he saw her raise the weapons. Gunfire danced across the floors and wall as he tried to escape. He reached into his pouch. The smoke bombs were still there.

He decided it was probably a good idea to get away from them before they destroyed the whole mall.

"There he is!" Bernie Bounder cried, jumping toward Billy as his monkey demon brothers followed.

"There I *was*," Billy retorted, throwing the smoke bombs down as hard as he could.

The bombs exploded; huge, billowing clouds of gray smoke escaped from the capsules to mask his retreat.

He hated to run but thought it best for the mall.

He played with the buttons on his goggles again, changing the lenses so that he could see through the smoke. He could make out the shapes of the Sassafrases and the Bounders searching for him, but he was able to avoid them, stealthily tiptoeing past the monsters on his way to the exit.

"He's in this smoke somewhere," he heard Sireena growl.

"We'll wait for the smoke to clear and then we'll find him," one of the Bounders suggested.

"Stupid monkey, do you think we have all day?"

Sireena screeched her displeasure. "Mother has a hair-dresser appointment in less than an hour."

"Then what do you suggest, troll woman?" another of the Bounders asked.

Billy reached the doors and stepped on the rubber mat that signaled them to swing open.

"I say we bring it down around his ears!" he heard Mother Sassafras cry out.

"Couldn't have said it better myself, Mother dear," Sireena agreed.

Suddenly the air was filled with the sound of explosions, and Billy found himself flung backward by the multiple blasts. He landed on his butt in the parking lot, just in front of the doors.

"Did you stop them?" one of the citizens waiting in the lot wanted to know. "Did you save our mall?"

He didn't have a chance to answer before the entire building began to tremble and shake, collapsing in upon itself and leaving only twisted rubble.

Billy picked himself up from the ground and turned toward those waiting in the lot. They were all standing perfectly still, eyes bulging in disbelief, mouths agape at what they had just witnessed.

"Whoops," Billy said.

* * *

It was a sold-out crowd at Giganticus Stadium.

The Puking Corpses were playing, their first concert in over one hundred fifty years, and somebody wanted to ruin it for the legion of dedicated Puking fans.

Not if I can help it, Archebold thought as he brought the bright yellow four-wheeler—the OwlWheeler—to a screeching stop in front of the entrance to the stadium.

Crowds loitered around outside the doors, hopeful Pukers desperate for tickets to the sold-out show.

Archebold revved the engine for effect before climbing from his vehicle.

"Look, it's Owlboy!" a woman with snakes for hair and wearing a Puking Corpses T-shirt cried. Before Archebold knew it, there was an eager crowd in front of him.

"Not Owlboy," the goblin corrected them. "OwlLad . . . it's different, you know."

"Figures Owlboy can get tickets to the show," complained a monster with too many teeth and a head like a grapefruit.

"It's Owl . . . *Lad*," Archebold stressed once more.

"I guess we'll just have to save Monstros a coupla times and then we can get anything we want," said another disgruntled Puking Corpses fan. "Oh, thank you soooooooooo much, Owlboy. You're better than anybody else."

"You misunderstand, good citizen," Archebold

attempted to explain. "First, it's OwlLad, and I haven't tickets to the show. I'm here to investigate a possible—"

Two fearsome monsters, all fangs and horns, wearing black T-shirts and Puking Corpses identification badges, emerged from the stadium, pushing the crowd aside.

Archebold was thinking that he was about to have a problem when one of the monsters spoke.

"The Corpses heard you were outside and would like you to join them onstage."

The goblin's smile was so wide it nearly split his face in two. He loved the Puking Corpses and had been a member of their fan club since their very first release, "Love till You Spew."

"Me?" he said with a girlish giggle. "The Corpses would like *me* to go up onstage with them?"

"You are Owlboy, correct?" the other beasties asked, leaning down to look through the goggles into his eyes.

"OwlLad," Archebold said, "but it's pretty much the same thing."

"Then come this way, sir," the monster said as he and the other beastie cut a path through the lingering crowds to get him inside the building.

"Hey, you guys haven't seen any villainy around here, have you?" Archebold asked as he was whisked down the snaking corridors and into a private elevator.

"There was an alarm going off at my supersecret head-quarters and—"

"No villainy," the monster to his left barked.

"Only the Puking Corpses," said the other, on Archebold's right.

Archebold shrugged. "Hmmm, must've been a false alarm."

Exiting the elevator, he allowed himself to be escorted down a winding corridor, the sounds of eager fans becoming louder and louder.

"Are we going in?" Archebold asked one of the black-garbed monsters.

"They want you onstage," the monster answered, directing him toward a closed metal door with a sign that read AUTHORIZED PERSONNEL ONLY.

"They want *me . . . onstage?*" Archebold gulped.

And before he knew it, he was whisked through the doors and bombarded with a cacophony of sound as the Puking Corpses rocked out onstage and the sold-out-stadium crowd roared with approval.

The lead singer of the Corpses, Vile, was dancing around the stage wearing his trademark black leather jumpsuit, singing one of their all-time-greatest hits, "If You Don't Love Me, Stab Me in the Eye."

Archebold couldn't believe his luck. He never would have imagined that he would be here, watching the real-live Vile performing with his favorite rock band.

As the lead guitarist, Rancid, began his earsplitting guitar solo, Vile looked backstage and saw Archebold standing there. The singer, his white face partially hidden by waves of long, stringy black hair, pointed to him with a skeletal finger.

Me? Archebold mouthed, turning around to be certain that nobody was standing behind him.

The rock star nodded his shaggy head enthusiastically, motioning for the goblin to come onto the stage to join them.

Archebold did.

"Ladies and gentlemen, we have a special guest with us tonight!" Vile announced. The crowd went mental. Rancid continued to play his part of the classic song, while the drummer, Rot Rogers, wailed on the elaborate drum set with multiple sets of arms all moving in different directions.

Archebold was completely paralyzed.

"The protector of Monstros City, the one, the only . . . *Owlboy!*"

The band went nuts, the last beats of their hit song and the cheers of the crowd blending together to form one deafening sound.

Vile then handed Archebold a microphone.

"It's Owl*Lad*," he corrected, and the sound of the crowd's approval grew even louder.

"So, Owlboy," Vile said, taking the microphone back. "What brings you to Giganticus Stadium . . . besides wanting to hear the sold-out Puking Corpses promote their greatest-hits collection, *Feeding the Worms*, which will be available in stores in two weeks?"

The crowd went mental again, and Archebold clapped, adding to the noise. He'd had no idea that the Corpses were putting out another greatest-hits collection this month.

Awesome!

The goblin took back the microphone from the lead singer.

"It's *Lad* . . . Owl*Lad*, and I'm actually here on superhero business," the superhero's sidekick said. The crowd was so worked up, Archebold figured he could say just about anything and get a wild response.

"And lima beans are awesome."

He was right: wild cheers, screams and whistles for lima beans.

Vile reached down and took the microphone from him again.

"That's so true, but before we sing another smash tune which will be available on our new greatest-hits record—hitting stores in two weeks—would you be willing to share with us what kind of superhero business it was that brought you to our sold-out concert tonight? Was it something totally cool?"

Vile held the microphone down so that Archebold could speak into it.

"Well, actually, I was responding to an alarm that a crime was being committed, but from what I can see, it must have been a false alarm."

Vile brought the microphone back to his own mouth.

"The only crime I see being committed here is that the Puking Corpses are rocking Monstros City like it's never been rocked before!"

The enthusiastic crowd whooped, shrieked and hollered again, and even Archebold found himself stamping his feet and hooting (as a sidekick to Owlboy should rightly do when excited) as Vile returned to the band to begin another song.

At first Archebold thought there was something on the lenses of his goggles, some kind of greenish grease. As he prepared to rock out, he tried to use one of his gloved fingers to wipe away the stain but was surprised to see that the lenses were actually clean.

"What the . . . ?" he muttered to himself as he watched a greenish cloud slowly drift down from the domed ceiling of the stadium.

And then he smelled it.

It was bad, really bad. Worse than a pile of three-week-old garbage. Worse than a bowl of tumor stew long forgotten at the back of the fridge. Even worse than the dirty diaper of an infant Stygian Bile Demon.

And then the whole arena smelled it, and things really began to get ugly.

Vile's face twisted up in disgust and he stopped singing. "What's that smell?" he asked before he began to cough and gag.

The audience was reacting to the sickening stench as well. They had begun to stampede toward the exits, trying to escape the most awful smell Archebold had ever encountered—and that was saying quite a bit, given that he had spent time with Halifax after the troll had eaten three yak tongue sandwiches.

That had been the worst stink ever.

Until now.

The greenish cloud was growing, hanging above the auditorium like a storm of stink.

And within the foul-smelling mist, for just a moment, Archebold thought he could see a ghostly shape.

It was smiling.

"Thanks a lot, Owlboy," Vile said between coughs as he and the Puking Corpses retreated from the stage. "Good job at protecting the greatest concert ever to rock the Giganticus Stadium in promotion of our new greatest-hits album hitting stores in two weeks."

"It's Owl*Lad*," Archebold corrected Vile, looking around to see that he was the only one left inside the stadium.

The supersonic skateboard, which Halifax liked to call the OwlSkate, zoomed up the driveway to the mansion of the mayor of Monstros City.

Halifax had originally designed the board for Billy's use, never expecting to be using it himself. But here he was, on a mission to save the mayor's home from harm.

The number-one goal of this mission—besides saving the mayor, of course—was to look cool. It was the Hooter's first time out in public, and he needed to do everything in his power to make sure he didn't embarrass himself.

The mansion loomed ahead. "OwlSkate, halt!" Halifax commanded, and the board immediately came to a screeching stop, causing him to fly from the deck and land in a crashing tumble in the driveway.

"Is that you, Owlboy?" a voice asked from somewhere close by.

Halifax climbed to his feet and pushed back his cape, which was now draped over his head.

"It's the Hooter," Halifax said. His goggles were askew, so he straightened them as he looked toward the mansion.

The mayor was at the window of one of the upstairs rooms. He was wearing a bright red bathrobe with a black velvet collar, and his ratlike features were twitching wildly as he raised his voice. "It took you long enough to get here. . . . Maybe I should have just called the Monstros City police instead!"

"What seems to be the problem, sir?" Halifax asked, trying to be polite. He would have rather told the rat-faced politician to go find himself another superhero to yell at, but he was aware that being courteous was part of the whole superheroing package.

"What seems to be the problem?" the mayor screeched, pointing to something behind the troll. "That giant robot seems to be the problem! I just had the front yard landscaped! Get that giant robot off my lawn!"

Halifax looked to see that, in fact, there *was* a giant robot standing on the mayor's lawn.

"Would you look at that," the troll mumbled to himself, strolling over to the robot. It was a good size, maybe twenty feet tall or so. It reminded him of some of the giant robots he'd designed and built over the years.

"Hello there," Halifax said to the motionless robot.

"Is there any reason why you're standing on the mayor's lawn?"

"I am a transporter," the robot suddenly droned, its eyes blazing yellow. "My function is to transport."

"Like a delivery?" Halifax asked. "Do you have some kind of delivery for the mayor?"

"Negative," the robot stated. "I have a delivery for Owlboy."

"Owlboy?" Halifax repeated, stepping back. "Well, he ain't here right now. Would a sidekick do?"

"I have a delivery for Owlboy," the robot stated again, eyes flashing.

"Well, I'm the Hooter; Owlboy and I are pretty close, and I'd be willing to accept this delivery, with the proper identification of course."

The robot started to shake and hum as two huge panels on its broad metal chest began to open.

Halifax reached for his tool belt and removed his greatest tool and weapon, his all-purpose wrench.

A platform lowered from the insides of the giant robot, and a small figure, even smaller than Archebold, waddled down to the mayor's lawn.

"What the heck is going on down there?" the mayor yelled from his window. "Hurry up and get that thing off my lawn. What the heck am I paying you for?"

"Paying? You don't pay us," Halifax answered, keeping his eye on the small creature that now stood before him.

"Oh," the mayor said. "Well, if I did, I'd ask for my money back."

"Well, don't get yourself all worked up for nothing," Halifax yelled up to the house. "I should have your problem taken care of pretty quick."

He leaned forward, talking down to the small, armored creature.

"And who might you be?" the troll asked in his kindest voice.

"Vomitor," the creature answered in a low, bubbling voice.

Halifax stood up, stroking his chin in thought. "Vomitor," he repeated. "Y'know, I think Owlboy once battled a supervillain with a name just like that."

"Vomitor," the armored creature repeated, the strange gurgling growing louder.

"Yep, Vomitor," Halifax agreed. "How about that? So, do you have something for Owlboy that you can give to me?"

"Vomitor," he answered.

"Yes, Vomitor, we're moving on from that now, thank you."

"Vomit—" he started again.

"That's enough of that, little guy," Halifax interrupted. "So what do you have for me?"

The armored creature motioned with a stubby, segmented finger for him to come closer.

"Yes?" Halifax asked.

Vomitor's mouth suddenly opened incredibly wide, and Halifax had to wonder if he'd ever seen a mouth able to open that much. And just when he was about ask why Vomitor had done that, the awful, strange, bubbling-gurgling sound grew louder.

Just as Halifax was about to put two and two together, Vomitor exploded.

Thick, bubbling, foul-smelling stomach juices flowed from the armored beastie's open maw. It was a tidal wave of nastiness that picked up Halifax and carried him across the mayor's property, right toward the house.

Helpless, caught up in the current of puke, Halifax watched in horror as the mayor's mansion came closer and closer, as did the mayor in his window, a tidal wave of foulness headed straight for him.

"You're fired!" the mayor screamed just before the wall of digestive juices struck the side of the mansion.

"I quit!" Halifax screamed, streaming through the window on a bubbling torrent of vomit.

CHAPTER 5

The Monarch stood before a row of eyeball-shaped monitors, watching secret footage of the villains at work.

"Interesting," he growled, stroking his chin with a gloved hand. "There appears to be more than one of them now."

Klot and Mukus moved in for a closer look.

"More than one Owlboy?" Mukus asked.

"Exactly," the Monarch answered. "Each of these disastrous events took place too close together for there to be only one." He pointed to each of the screens as the superheroes' failures played out over and over again.

"Son of a gun," Klot said. "All this time he was cheating."

"No," the Monarch corrected, his eyes riveted to the screens. "I believe this is a more recent turn of events. There is still only one real Owlboy; these buffoons are probably . . . lackeys."

He turned his hooded head to look at his own.

"Lackeys," Mukus repeated with a snarl. "I hate those guys."

Klot nodded. "Yeah, me too."

Within his hood, the Monarch rolled his eyes. It was tough to get good lackeys these days, and it was never more obvious than during conversations like this.

There was a sudden flash of white, and they all turned toward the center of the room.

The villains were returning from their missions with the help of miniature teleportation devices the Monarch had created for them.

"Excellent job," the Monarch proclaimed as the villains recovered from the effects of the teleporting. "I applaud you all."

And the master crime lord of Monstros did, bringing his black-gloved hands together.

"We could have killed him," Sireena growled, hefting her weapon and shaking it at the ceiling.

"You demolished an entire mall. I would think that would be enough to momentarily satisfy your blood-lust," the Monarch said.

"The only thing that's gonna satisfy me is blasting Owlboy into little pieces," Sireena insisted, pretending to fire her gun into an imaginary something lying on the ground.

Mother Sassafras smiled, patting her daughter on the head. "That's my girl," the troll mother said, beaming. "She makes me so proud." She began to sniffle and wiped her dripping nose on the sleeve of her dress.

"I could have filled his lungs with noxious gas and choked the life from him," the Ghost said, floating above the room.

"And we could have stomped him into owl juice," Balthasar Bounder said as all his demon monkey brothers eagerly nodded.

"To digest his heroic form in my stomach juices," the armored Vomitor gurgled, "would have been a most glorious thing." His huge mouth bent into a smile.

"But it would have been over all too quickly," the Monarch stated.

"So what?" Sigmund asked. "Owlboy would be dead, and that would be that. We'd be free to perform any act of villainy we wanted."

"Now, where's the fun in that?" the Monarch asked.

"Owlboy's suffering must be long and drawn-out . . . savored like a fine glass of Jugular Wine."

The leader of the villains turned to his eyeball televisions and produced a remote from one of the pockets of his robe. He aimed the remote at the televisions and one by one they began to change.

"An instant death is far too merciful," the Monarch stated.

Each television showed a different news program, and they were all talking about Owlboy and his failures.

"He must be made to suffer before we destroy him completely."

Billy had been the first to arrive back at the Roost. He'd returned the rocket pack to storage in the garage and then gone up into the headquarters to find the others and report his failure, but they hadn't returned yet.

Zis-Boom-Bah and Ferdinand were excited to see him, obviously unaware of how badly he'd screwed up at the mall.

The miniaturized monster with the upper body of a gorilla, the antennae of a bug, the lower body of a dinosaur and the tail of a fish hugged Billy's lower leg lovingly while Ferdinand the dragon flew circles around his head.

"Hey, guys," Billy said in greeting. "Nobody else is back yet, huh?"

The tiny monsters responded with a series of grunts and squeaks that Billy really didn't understand, but he got the message: he was the first one to arrive back at the Roost.

From a pouch on his utility belt Billy removed the communicator Halifax had given him and turned it on. All he got was static that hurt his ears. He'd tried to use it after the mall had collapsed, to let Archebold know what had happened, but he hadn't been able to get through to him, or to Halifax, for that matter.

He hoped they were having better luck than he'd had.

And with that thought, Billy heard the elevator coming up from the garage. At the end of the hallway, the doors on the elevator slid open, and Archebold stepped out in his OwlLad costume. But he wasn't the only thing that came out of the elevator.

The goblin wasn't even halfway down the corridor when the smell flooded into the monitor room.

"Oh my God," Billy said, clamping a hand over his mouth and nose. "What's that smell?"

"It's the smell of defeat," Archebold said, his shoulders slumped.

The tiny monsters were excited to see Archebold as well, until they got too close.

"What happened to you?" Billy asked through his hand, afraid to breathe.

Archebold pulled out a chair and sat down heavily.

"It was going so well," he explained. "I got to the stadium and was asked to go onstage with the Puking Corpses. Then some stinky ghost had to go and pollute the entire place with his stench!"

"A ghost?" Billy asked.

The goblin nodded, removing his helmet and goggles. "A ghost made from some kind of stinky green gas."

The door from the shadow paths then flew open and they both watched as Halifax came into the room. He was carrying the OwlSkate beneath his arms, and his costume appeared to be soaking wet and covered in . . . something too gross to even mention.

"I don't want to talk about it!" the troll yelled as he slammed the door.

"Don't tell me," Billy said. "You failed on your mission, too."

Halifax wiped some drying spew from his goggles. "Why, did you guys have a bad time?"

Both Billy and Archebold slowly nodded.

"The whole mall collapsed," Billy said, looking to Archebold.

"The Puking Corpses concert had to be evacuated because of a ghostly stink."

"Is that you?" Halifax asked, holding his nose. "I thought I was starting to smell worse than I already did."

"What happened to you?" Billy asked the troll.

"I had a run-in with some armored villain called Vomitor," he explained.

"Dude, is that . . . ?" Billy started to ask, wrinkling his nose in disgust as he pointed to the stuff dripping from Halifax's Hooter costume.

"I think it is," Archebold answered, sadly shaking his head. "Oh, how the mighty have fallen."

Billy couldn't believe it; it was bad enough that he had failed, but his two sidekicks, too? Add that to what had happened at school and it was official—this was the worst day of his life.

"So I went up against the Bounder boys and the Sassafras family," he said, pointing to himself. "Archebold went up against a really stinky ghost, and Halifax was puked on by somebody called Vomitor."

His friends nodded.

"What's up with that?" Billy asked. "Were they giving get-out-of-jail-free cards over at Beelzebub?"

Archebold snapped his fingers. "I knew there was something I wanted to tell you," the goblin said. "There was a prison break the other night."

"And you forgot?" Billy asked, annoyed.

"I don't know if *forgot* is the right word," the goblin said, looking to Halifax for support.

"*Screwed up royally* comes to my mind," the troll said.

"Don't sweat it," Billy said. "We would've gotten our butts kicked tonight anyway."

Halifax picked up the OwlSkate and slung it over his shoulder. "I don't know about you, but I could use some snacks," he said.

They all agreed that was the thing to lift their spirits, but Archebold and Halifax definitely had to clean up first.

An hour later, Billy, Archebold and Halifax were in the snack room, gorging themselves on bloodberry pie, cockroach-chunk ice scream, country-fried pterodactyl and whatever else they could find to chase away the blues.

"I can't believe we all fouled up so bad," Archebold said, popping a handful of chocolate-covered newt eyeballs in his mouth.

"Maybe we're just not cut out to be sidekicks," Halifax added, breaking off some crust from his bloodberry pie and giving it to Zis-Boom-Bah.

"Don't you think it was kinda weird, that stuff all

happening at once?" Billy asked. Ferdinand was asleep in his lap, and he gently stroked the slumbering dragon's scales.

"It was a little odd," Archebold agreed. "You thinking there's something more to it than a nasty coincidence?"

"I'm not sure," Billy said. "It's kind of like somebody's trying to test Owlboy . . . trying to stretch him to his limits." Billy had a big swig from a bubbling glass of poltergeist potion. "Just a thought."

Halifax pushed his empty pie plate toward a waiting Zis-Boom-Bah.

"Something to keep in mind," Archebold said, "but I think right now we just need to kick back and relax a bit." The goblin, seated in an overstuffed recliner, reached down between the cushion and the chair frame, coming up with a remote control. "How's about a little TV?" he suggested.

They all thought this was a good idea. Billy hadn't seen much television in Monstros and was curious about the kind of programming they had.

Archebold pointed the large remote at one of the portraits of a previous Owlboy that decorated the walls of the snack room, and pushed a button. With a low hum, the picture rose to reveal a good-sized television screen beneath. It wasn't a fifty-inch plasma like the one Billy's great-aunt Tilly could watch at Shady Acres, but it was a pretty decent size.

"So, what's on?" Billy asked, getting excited.

"Not sure," Archebold said, turning the set on.

"*Bowling for Organs* is good," Halifax said. "I hear somebody could win a new pancreas today."

The TV came on in the middle of a news report.

An attractive monster—as far as monsters go—was reporting in front of the rubble of the Monstros City Mall.

"Oh my gosh, it's the mall!" Billy cried, moving to the edge of his seat, his sudden movement waking up the sleeping Ferdinand. "What's she saying?"

"That's Violet Venomous," Halifax said. "She's one of the top investigative reporters in Monstros."

They all moved closer to the television.

"Nobody knows for sure what happened, but what is known is that the Monstros City mall, once one of the city's crown jewels of commerce, is now nothing more than a pile of twisted wreckage thanks to someone who was once considered our protector and savior . . . Owlboy."

Billy and the gang gasped. Ferdinand rose to all fours and growled at the television, small gouts of orange flame shooting from her nostrils.

Violet began to interview some mall shoppers.

"What happened here today?" she asked the creature wrapped in filthy bandages.

"I talked to her!" Billy yelled at the set. Archebold and Halifax shushed him.

"We thought he'd come to save us, but I guess we were wrong," the bandaged beastie said with a sad shake of its head. "It's a real shame, I liked this mall."

Billy gulped as Violet interviewed another.

"All I wanted was some hand cream," a giant worm wearing a hockey helmet said before breaking down into pitiful sobs.

"Hand cream?" Halifax asked.

The ugly little creature with the huge handbag was the next to be interviewed.

"He took my Dr. Mellman's Home Surgery Kit," she said, eyes bulging. "Said he'd been looking everywhere for one and took mine. It's a crime, I tell you!"

Billy jumped to his feet. "She's a big fat liar!" he screamed, shaking a finger at the screen.

"All right, calm down," Archebold said, turning the channel.

But it appeared that there was no escaping their really bad night. Another news program was reporting from the Giganticus Stadium about the evacuated Puking Corpses concert.

"Oh no," Archebold said as another reporter, a giant

squid, placed multiple microphones in front of multiple Puking Corpses fans who had been forced to leave the show.

"It's all Owlboy's fault. I think he ate something nasty before he got here."

"The stink was so bad you could bang nails into it."

"At first I thought it was all part of the show, y'know, like Smellavision? But then I threw up."

Halifax reached over and snatched the remote away.

"You guys don't need to be seeing that stuff," the troll said quickly, turning the channel to something hopefully less disturbing.

The ratlike face of the mayor of Monstros filled the screen.

"Aaaaah!" Halifax shrieked. He dropped the remote to the floor and fumbled to retrieve it.

The mayor was in the middle of a rant . . . a rant against Owlboy.

"He calls himself a hero?" the politician screeched into the microphones. "Well, I call him a menace. It's going to take months and a small fortune to clean all the spew out of my mansion . . . and that, I'm afraid, is going to result in higher taxes."

Zis-Boom-Bah stomped on the remote, turning the television off and plunging the room into silence.

Nobody, it seemed, knew what to say.

"I guess it could be worse," Archebold said with a nervous chuckle.

"Worse?" Billy asked. "Did you see what I just saw? They hate us."

"Correction," Halifax said. "They hate you."

Billy slapped a hand over his face. "I can't imagine a worse day."

But then he remembered what still waited for him at school tomorrow.

The sad thing was, it was only going to get worse.

Billy woke up the next morning feeling like a failure.

It was the first real defeat he'd experienced since taking on the mantle of Owlboy, and it had left him feeling just awful.

He got up, washed his failure face, put on his failure clothes, went downstairs and had a big bowl of failure flakes and then picked up his book bag full of failure and went to school, where he was pretty sure he was going to fail some more.

By second period, he'd sat through two classes but hadn't failed at anything else. Things weren't quite so bad.

Yet.

Third period was when the poop hit the jet engine.

Mr. Harpin had called all his science classes together in the school auditorium, breaking them down into their teams so that they could decide on topics for their project.

Billy felt like a bloody piece of steak thrown to a cage full of hungry velociraptors.

"So, Billy boy, any ideas?" Randy asked with a jagged, jack-o'-lantern-sized grin.

Billy shrugged, staring stupidly at the three subhumans who sat in the seats around him.

"Nothing?" Randy asked. "That's weird. I woulda thought you had something all worked up and ready to go."

Billy shrugged again, examining a black speck stuck beneath his thumbnail.

Penny blew an enormous bubble, let it pop and peeled it from her face with her baby-poop-green claws.

"Well, somebody better come up with something," she said, and scowled, reminding Billy a little bit of Sireena Sassafras. "I hate science and I'm not gonna do it."

"I'm pretty sure I had a project," Darious said, eyes darting around the auditorium. "But something made me forget it."

"Huh," Mitchell said, giving Darious the hairy eyeball. "Imagine that."

The boy nodded. "Yeah, probably the government—they've stolen a bunch of my ideas before."

"It's a good thing Mitchell and I have been talking, Hooten," Randy said.

Billy looked up into his archenemy's cavemanlike face.

"You two have come up with an idea for a project?"

Randy and Mitchell nodded.

"Don't say that too loud," Darious said, quickly looking around. "The walls have ears."

Randy ignored him. "Yesterday me and Mitchell saw a squirrel get run over by a truck and it got my gears going."

"It really did," Mitchell said, and started to laugh.

"After I saw the squirrel buy it, I said to Mitchell, hey, Mitchell, we should kill something and bring it back to life with electricity for our science project. We could be like Frankenstein, only not German."

"And I said awesome," Mitchell added excitedly.

"That's totally sick," Billy said, his face crinkled up in disgust.

"Why?" Mitchell asked. "It would only be dead for a little while."

"You're both insane," Billy said. "It doesn't work like that."

"Does in the movies," Randy answered as Mitchell,

Penny and Darious nodded. It was obvious that they all liked the idea.

Big surprise.

"Idiots," Billy muttered beneath his breath. He had more ideas for science projects than he knew what to do with, but he refused to let these morons have any of them. They were his, and nobody—especially a gang with the accumulated IQ of a snow cone—was going to steal them from him.

"What did you just call us?" Mitchell asked, standing up and glaring at Billy.

Billy refused to answer, picking at the spot beneath his nail again.

"Y'know, we could skip the animal part altogether and kill one of the team instead," Randy suggested.

Billy felt their eyes on him then, and swallowed with a loud gulp. Then out of the corner of his eye, he caught movement as Mr. Harpin made his way down the aisle toward them.

"I noticed you people in the midst of heated discussion," the science teacher said, pulling his eyeglasses from his shirt pocket and putting them on. He studied a piece of paper on a clipboard, making notes here and there. "So I'm guessing you have a topic that will knock my socks off."

He paused, waiting for them to answer.

Billy didn't want to open his mouth. In fact, he sent

a special mental message to his vocal cords commanding them not to move. Unfortunately, they didn't listen, and he knew immediately that his mouth and his vocal cords had teamed up with his brain to undermine his authority.

"Our project is on the eruption of Mount Vesuvius and its effects on Pompeii."

Mr. Harpin nodded. "Fascinating." He took some more notes.

"Glad you like it, sir," Randy said. "We really had to rack our brains to come up with something unique."

"Really unique," Mitchell said, nodding.

Billy thought he was going to throw up.

"Even though I hate science," Penny said in between gum snaps, "I totally helped come up with this totally awesome idea."

"I don't think it's as good as the one that the government stole from me, but it has to be a close second," Darious commented.

Billy could only sit and fume.

Mr. Harpin finished writing his notes and looked up. "This is an excellent idea," he stated. "And I'm counting on this team to knock it out of the park."

"Oh, we will, sir," Randy said, reaching over to smack Billy in the shoulder. "We're all about the team, right, Bill?"

It hurt like heck, but Billy forced a smile.

"Now, you're all aware that we have an accelerated deadline for the completion of these projects, right?" Mr. Harpin asked.

"Accelerated deadline?" Billy squeaked.

"Yes, you know, to be part of the statewide competition."

"So when is the project due?"

"Next week."

"Next week?" Billy screamed.

The science teacher looked at him and smiled. "Why, Mr. Hooten, it seems to me like you've got a team that will work together like a well-oiled machine. You shouldn't have any problem getting this done by the deadline."

And he turned away, moving on to the next team.

Billy couldn't move. He felt as though he'd been poisoned by the deadly quills of a lion-fish. His entire body started to shut down.

"A week," Randy said with a slow nod.

"Looks like you've got an awful lot of work to do, Hooten," he added. "Better get crackin'."

CHAPTER 6

Back in Monstros City, things at the Roost weren't going much better.

Archebold scanned the front of the *Monstros City Times*, reading the painful headline on the latest edition of the newspaper. HERO OR MENANCE? it asked in large black letters, alongside a photo of Billy taken at the parade given for Owlboy after he'd saved Monstros from Zis-Boom-Bah a few weeks back.

"This is just too painful," the goblin said, setting the paper down on a pile of others, each displaying similar headlines.

Halifax was looking at the newest magazines to hit the stands, flipping through the latest issue of *Wagging Tongue*.

It wasn't very pretty.

"It says here that Owlboy has been hitting the joy juice, which is why he fouled up those last three missions." The troll set the magazine down. "That actually explains a lot," he said.

Archebold reached across the table and smacked Halifax on the side of his shaggy head.

"What's the matter with you?" he screeched.

"What!" Halifax cried, raising his arms to block any further violence.

"Joy juice? You actually believe this nonsense they're printing about Billy?" Archebold asked in disbelief. "Are you forgetting that we're partially to blame for his troubles?"

"Oh yeah," Halifax said. "For a minute there, I was almost caught up in all the scandal."

Archebold slapped his wrinkly forehead. "Scandal? There is no scandal. . . . Owlboy had a bad day, that's it in a nutshell."

"Coulda fooled me," Halifax said sadly, lifting a stack of gossip magazines that all had something nasty to say about the hero.

Ferdinand swooped by and blasted the stack of magazines with a gout of orange flame, incinerating the bad news.

"Atta girl, Ferdinand," Archebold praised the dragon.

Zis-Boom-Bah had climbed up onto the table and was tearing up the newspapers and growling savagely . . . well, as savagely as ten inches of monster could.

"You guys have the right idea," the goblin said as the tiny dragon perched on his head.

"So what're we gonna do?" Halifax asked despondently. "I can fix just about anything, but I can't fix this. It's very frustrating."

"I know," Archebold agreed. "We've got to rack our brains and come up with a way to get Owlboy back in the city's good graces."

They sat in silence, the smell of burning plastic filling the air as they strained their thinking muscles.

"I've got it," Halifax said with a snap of his callused fingers.

Archebold's eyes gleamed in anticipation.

"We throw a dance and invite everyone," the troll said. "Everybody loves to dance. We'll have food and everything."

Archebold just stared.

"What?" Halifax asked. "Is it too much?"

"A dance would never work," the goblin said, stroking his rounded chin. Suddenly his eyes bugged and his long ears began to twitch. "But what about a bake sale?"

"That's a great idea!" Halifax said, jumping up from his chair.

A violent tremor shook the Roost.

"What the heck was that?" Archebold asked, grabbing hold of the table to keep from being shaken from his chair.

Halifax looked around as multiple security alarms began to clang, clatter and hoot. "Oh jeez," he said. "I've never heard that alarm before."

"What alarm?" Archebold asked as another shock wave went through the secret location.

"The invasion alarm," the troll said, looking around the room.

"Invasion alarm?" Archebold repeated.

"Yes! The Roost is being invaded!"

Halifax's eyes grew really big and locked on to Archebold's, which were also quite large.

"The Roost is being invaded!" they screamed in unison as the giant tree continued to tremble and shake.

And then something exploded through the floor.

Sireena Sassafras wanted to kill something.

The troll supervillain wasn't used to working with a team. It was hard enough working with her brother and her mother, but now she was being forced to work with a foul-smelling ghost, filthy bouncing monkeys and a guy who threw up at the drop of a hat.

Killing something wouldn't make working with this

team of losers any easier, but it would sure make her feel better.

The first to emerge from the tunnel they had dug through the earth and finally up into the ginormous old tree, Sireena tossed the atomic digging tool given to her by the Monarch onto the floor of the Roost.

"This is his secret hideout?" she asked, looking around, her face twisted with distaste. "What a dump."

"Help your mother!" Mother Sassafras wailed from within the hole.

Sireena bent down, took one of her mother's large hands in her own and gave a powerful tug.

"A lady shouldn't be forced to crawl through dirty holes, especially in my delicate condition," the troll woman said as she emerged. "She should be at home in front of a fire doing lady things, like skinning cats and hollowing out skulls to make decorative decanters."

"You can do your arts and crafts after we've ruined Owlboy for good," Sireena told her.

"I guess you're right," Mother Sassafras agreed, plucking at her giant stack of hair with a clawed hand. It resembled some sort of weird sculpture.

The filthy monkey Bounder boys bounced from the hole into the room, chattering away, with Vomitor, the Gaseous Ghost and Sireena's brother right behind them.

94

"So where is he?" Sigmund asked, wiping dust and dirt from his clothes and unslinging his high-powered rifle from his shoulder. "If this is his secret hideout, then where's Owlboy?"

"Maybe he's out getting milk?" Bobby Bounder suggested.

"Or out for dinner with some friends?" offered Bernie.

"Maybe he's taking a ceramics class," Bailey considered. "I've always wanted a ceramic cookie jar. I wonder if he'd make me one if I offered to pay him."

"If you offered to pay, I can't see why he wouldn't," Balthasar said.

"Vomitor bet he wouldn't mind," Vomitor added.

"You don't think so? I've been dying to have a jar that looks like a pig, with blue overalls and a straw hat that you lift up to get at the cookies inside his—"

Sireena couldn't take it anymore.

"Enough about the cookie jar!" she screamed, resisting the urge to skin the monkeys and make them into a lovely fur vest.

"All this talk about cookies makes me want some," Bobby Bounder said.

"We should try to find some," Balthasar agreed.

The Gaseous Ghost floated above their heads on a wave of stink. "The female Sassafras is correct," he said.

"Owlboy is a superhero; he wouldn't make you a pig cookie jar even if you paid him twice."

"I didn't . . . ," Sireena began, but decided against finishing her statement. She seriously began to entertain the thought of murdering all of them, wondering how drastic the repercussions would be from her new employer.

With that thought, she looked around the room again. The Monarch was supposed to be meeting them here for further instructions, but he didn't seem to be around.

"I see you have arrived," said an all-too-familiar voice from multiple sets of speakers. A wall of television sets across the room suddenly went to static, then to an image of the Monarch sitting in his elaborate throne.

"Excellent," the Monarch hissed. "Have you found Owlboy yet?"

"I don't think he's around," Sireena said, moving closer to the screens. "Can't imagine that he wouldn't have come running once he knew we'd entered."

"We think he's at ceramics," Bailey Bounder said, coming to stand beside her.

With a snarl, Sireena grabbed the monkey demon by the head and tossed him across the room.

"Perhaps he isn't here," she suggested to the

Monarch, regaining her composure. "Perhaps he isn't even in Monstros."

"Good point," the crime lord allowed.

"Perhaps he has returned to the world of humans above," she added.

Sireena heard a ruckus behind her and turned to see her mother swaying.

"The world of humans," the large troll woman said, throwing an arm dramatically across her brow. "Just the thought of that horrible, horrible place . . . I think I'm going to faint."

Sigmund ran to catch his mother but instead was knocked to the ground, trapped beneath her enormous weight.

Sireena looked back to the television screens.

"Sorry about that," she said. "My brother and I once paid a visit to the human world in pursuit of Owlboy and told her all about it."

"Quite all right," the Monarch said. "An interesting theory, though. If he has gone to the world above, we must see to it that he isn't allowed to come back."

Sireena tilted her head quizzically to one side. "And how would we do that?"

"Take your family and your favorite weapons and guard the shadow paths," the Monarch instructed.

"Prevent Owlboy from returning to Monstros until the damage is already done."

The Bounders and Vomitor were attempting to lift Mother Sassafras from atop Sigmund as the Ghost supervised the operation from above.

"And if my brother, mother and I are guarding the shadow paths, what of the others?"

"They will do what villains do best," The Monarch said. "They will cause complete and total chaos."

"I think I'm going to pee my overalls," Halifax whispered from inside one of the heating ducts. He and Archebold were peering down through a vent at the villains that had invaded their home.

As soon as the hole had opened in the floor, Archebold had known they had big-time trouble with a capital T. He'd dragged his friends to the first hiding place he could think of.

"Don't you dare," Archebold warned softly. "You'll drown us for sure."

Ferdinand and Zis-Boom-Bah looked out through the vent at the bad guys and began to growl.

"Hush, guys," Archebold whispered. "We can't let them know we're here."

"What're we gonna do?" Halifax asked. "We can't

stay here. . . . I hate cramped spaces—it feels like the walls are closing in on me."

"Would you rather be down there with the ugly club?" Archebold asked.

"You've got a point," the troll answered. "It is sort of cozy here."

"Well, don't get too comfortable, because I'm already thinking about what we have to do next."

"And that is?" Halifax asked.

"We have to warn Billy."

"And how, pray tell, are we going to do that while we're trapped in a heating duct?"

"You of all people know that these ducts go all over the inside of the Roost," Archebold explained.

"Go on," Halifax urged. "I'm fascinated."

"Well, we'll crawl through the ducts to get us just outside the Roost and use the shadow paths to get to Billy to let him know what's up."

"But what about the Sassafrases?" Halifax asked nervously. "Whoever is down there giving orders told them to guard the shadow paths."

"Then we'll just have to be extracareful so they don't catch us," Archebold explained. He looked at the two little monsters. "I want you two to stay here and keep an eye on things, but stay out of trouble."

The two beasties nodded, but something told

Archebold that staying out of trouble just wasn't in their repertoire.

Reluctantly, he and Halifax headed out through the ducts.

It felt as though they'd crawled through thousands of miles of heating ducts, and both were anxious to get to Billy.

"How about this one?" Halifax finally asked, peering out a vent into a dark corridor.

Archebold crawled up beside him and took a peek.

"I think this is good," the goblin said. "If I remember right, the staircase up to the human world is right over there." Archebold pointed as Halifax nodded. "Are you ready for this?"

"As ready as I'll ever be, I guess," the troll answered. "Hey, Archebold, how do you think those bad guys found the Roost anyway? I thought it was super-secret."

"Me too," Archebold answered, troubled by Halifax's comments. "And who was Sireena Sassafras talking to on our monitor screens?"

"Got me again," Halifax said with a shrug.

"Mysteries that we'll have to solve after we warn Billy," Archebold said. He pointed to the vent. "Do your stuff, pally."

With those words, Halifax produced a screwdriver

from the bib pocket of his overalls and removed the screws that kept the vent cover locked in place.

"I'll go first," Archebold told him, putting the cover aside.

"Be careful," Halifax warned as he watched him drop out of the vent to the shadow path.

Archebold landed in a squat and carefully checked out his surroundings.

"The coast is clear," the goblin whispered up to his friend.

Halifax climbed from the vent, letting his feet dangle for a moment before he dropped to the corridor of shadow below.

Archebold placed a stubby finger to his mouth. "Let's keep the voices down just in case," he said, motioning for Halifax to follow. "C'mon, the stairs are right over—"

The two scuttled around a corner in the blackness and practically ran into the backs of the Sassafras family.

Archebold and Halifax froze. The three evil trolls hadn't yet noticed them.

"Are you sure the battery is charged on this thing?" Mother Sassafras asked, giving a nasty-looking blaster pistol a shake.

"Yes, I'm sure, Mother," Sigmund answered, trying

to take the weapon from her hand. "I charged it myself last night, and you need to be careful with it before you—"

Fzzappp!

A bolt of crackling power shot from the gun, striking Sireena—who had been trying to touch up her makeup—in her rather large buttocks. The shadow passage was suddenly filled with the strangely succulent aroma of roasting pig.

"*Yeoowch!*" the female sibling roared, her tiny mirror flying from her hand.

"I guess you were right," Mother Sassafras told her son, eyeing the weapon with an approving nod.

"Why should I not destroy the both of you?" Sireena bellowed, pointing her own weapon menacingly at her mother and brother.

"That would be something, eh, Archebold?" Halifax said in a normal-sounding voice. "Let them take themselves out and Billy wouldn't have to do a thing."

The Sassafrases turned as one toward them.

"Did I say that too loud?" Halifax asked.

Archebold slowly shook his head. "Some days I just don't know about you." He reached out and grabbed his troll buddy by the arm. "Run like the dickens!" he shrieked, heading straight for the awful family.

"Get them!" Sireena screamed, trying to aim down

the barrel of her weapon, but Archebold and Halifax were moving too fast, right toward Mother Sassafras.

"I'll get them," the giant troll bellowed, pointing her blaster at the pair.

"Under the bridge!" Archebold screamed as he dragged Halifax between the giant troll mother's legs.

"That was amazing!" Halifax gasped, jumping up to run alongside him.

"We're not out of the woods yet," the goblin said, his short legs pumping like mad. "We've got to get to the steps up to the surface."

Beams of crackling yellow power struck the ground and walls of the passage as the Sassafras family chased them.

"Stop running so that we can kill you!" Sigmund ordered, firing off multiple shots that temporarily illuminated a section of the path.

"Right over there," Archebold said, steering Halifax toward the stone stairway to the world of humans above.

"Those guys give trolls a bad name," Halifax said, quickly glancing over his shoulder to see if the evil family was still after them.

Of course they were.

"C'mon, start climbing," Archebold said, pushing his buddy in front of him to begin the trek upward.

"Do you think they'll try to follow us?" Halifax asked breathlessly.

"Don't know," Archebold said, and he craned his neck slightly, looking down at the stairs they'd already climbed. He could hear the Sassafrases coming around the bend, arguing among themselves.

Suddenly Sireena appeared, aiming her rifle at them. "There they are!" she screeched, her voice like talons scraping down a sheet of glass.

Her brother and mother attempted to squeeze into the passage behind her.

Archebold was trying to push Halifax up the stairs with all his might, but the troll was tired and his legs were slowing down.

"Y'gotta move, buddy," Archebold cried.

Halifax tried, but just wasn't fast enough.

The Sassafras family fired their weapons all at once, the beams of destructive light striking the steps and walls of concentrated shadow around them.

Halifax and Archebold managed to avoid getting hit, but then the unthinkable happened. Just as they were beginning to climb the steps again, the shadowy substance that made up the staircase began to crumble.

Try as they might, they weren't fast enough to move themselves up the crumbling bits. They found themselves suddenly falling.

Down into shadow darker than any shadow had the right to be.

Billy pushed his plate of Chinese food away. He was hungry enough to have had at least two more helpings of sesame chicken, but there just wasn't the time. He had to try to accomplish something on his science fair assignment tonight.

"Don't you want your fortune cookie?" his mom asked.

"Already know my fortune," he said as he started up the stairs two at a time. "It'll say 'You will work, work, work and then do some more work just in case you haven't worked enough' . . . or something to that effect."

He headed to his room, going right for his desk and his stack of notes. It killed him to be sharing a project, especially something as cool as the Vesuvius project. In fact, he would hate to share any of his many awesome ideas for this year's science fair.

He plopped into his desk chair with a sigh and grabbed the stack of papers. Sifting through the stack, past all kinds of notes on all kinds of cool science experiments, he finally found what he was looking for. He decided to start a list of all that he had to do to make this project happen.

It would have been a whole lot easier if his team were actually going to help him. For a second he thought about telling on Randy and the others, turning them all in to Mr. Harpin, but he didn't feel like spending any time in the hospital with multiple broken bones.

Remembering Cole's story about finding at least one thing you liked about something you didn't want to do, Billy threw himself into a drawing of Vesuvius and the city of Pompeii beneath it. If he could get the actual model to look half as good as this blueprint, he was golden.

Billy was coloring in the rivers of lava flowing toward the Italian city when he heard the ruckus outside. Going to the window, he realized that the noise was coming from inside the garage.

He was immediately worried. He kept his coolest stuff in the garage, and didn't want anything—animal, vegetable or mineral—fooling around with it.

He left his room, went downstairs and found his father in the hallway. His dad was brandishing a golf club as if it were Excalibur itself.

"Did you hear that?" he asked Billy.

Billy's mother was still sitting on the love seat, an afghan pulled up to her face. "What do you think it is?" she asked. "It's not burglars, is it? Do you think it could be burglars? Maybe I should dial 911." She started to get up.

"Don't," Dad ordered, pointing the nine iron in her direction. "Billy and I are going to see what's up." He nodded to Billy and they made their way ever so carefully into the kitchen. "It's probably just a raccoon," his father said, opening the door.

"Or some kind of monkey," Billy added, his imagination getting the better of him.

Dad stopped and turned to him. "A monkey? Why would there be a monkey loose in our garage in Bradbury, Massachusetts?"

Billy shrugged. "Maybe a circus train derailed and all the animals got loose."

His father shook his head and continued down the steps.

"The monkey could be some kind of specially trained monkey . . . maybe an assistant to the knife thrower! And he's in our garage right now sharpening his knives so that—"

"Do you mind?" his father asked, about to unlock the garage door.

"Sorry," Billy said. "Sometimes I just can't turn it off." His dad grunted as he pulled the door open and raised his golf club.

Slowly they both stepped inside. It was pitch-black,

the light from the front porch of the house providing the only illumination.

"Turn on the light," his dad commanded, poised to strike if necessary.

Billy fished for the switch, his hand sliding over the surface of the wall. Just as he was about to flick the switch, a strange buzzing sound filled the air.

"What's that?" Billy asked, pulling his hand back.

"I don't know," his dad said.

Just then something flew at them out of the darkness—something that glowed a fiery orange.

"*Arrrgh!*" his father screamed, swinging the golf club like a deranged Jedi Knight.

"*Arrreeeiiiiiii!*" Billy screamed, ducking to get out of his father's way.

It was some kind of bug, a giant glowing bug, and his father was doing everything in his power to swat it from the air. "It's some kind of bird!" he yelled, swinging wildly, knocking over a box of Christmas dishes that smashed on the floor. "Maybe a vulture!"

Billy knew it wasn't a vulture. As he watched the large shape buzz and dart around, he suddenly realized *who* it was flying inside his garage.

The glow from the insect went dark and the buzzing abruptly stopped.

His father stood tensed, ready for action that didn't

seem to be coming. Finally, he fumbled for the light. Billy held his breath, not sure what they would see.

Nothing.

"I think it flew past us and out the door," Dad said, finally lowering his guard as well as his nine iron. "Wonder what the heck a vulture was doing inside our garage." He poked around with the golf club, making sure that whatever it was had indeed gone. "Guess we took care of that." His puffed out his chest proudly. "Let's go tell Mom that we vanquished our foe."

"You go tell her," Billy said. "I've got to get some supplies for my science fair project."

His dad looked around the room again. "Sure you'll feel safe enough?"

Billy nodded. "I'll be fine."

His dad took one last look around before handing Billy the golf club. "Better take this," he said. "You know, just in case."

Billy took it, smiling. "Thanks."

"Lock up the garage before you come in," his father said as he went into the house.

Billy could hear his mother just inside the door, asking what was going on, saying that she had heard a crash. Dad was telling her about the vulture that had attacked him and how it had first knocked over the Christmas dishes.

The door closed on his mother's shriek.

Billy reached over and turned off the light. It was wicked bright, and he knew that things from Monstros were scared by that much light.

He was looking for an insect—firefly, to be precise.

A firefly that went by the name of Walter.

"Hey, Walter, was that you?" Billy called out, looking around the garage, golf club in hand. "Hey!"

A section of the garage suddenly became illuminated with an orange glow. It came from behind a stack of boxes filled with old coats that his mom promised to donate to charity every year but never got around to packing up.

Billy spotted Walter, the firefly's backside glowing brightly as he directed his light toward the shapes of Archebold and Halifax.

The two looked terrified.

"What the heck are you guys doing in here?" Billy asked.

"It's bad, Billy. Really, really bad," Archebold said. Halifax just stood there and trembled.

Billy felt his heartbeat quicken. "Is there something wrong in Monstros?" he asked.

They both nodded vigorously, until Halifax finally got the courage to speak. "The bad guys . . . the ones that kicked our butts . . . they're back and they attacked the Roost—"

"And are gonna ruin Monstros to try to get everybody to hate you," Archebold added.

"They already hate me," Billy said.

"They want folks to hate you even more," Halifax explained. "If you can believe it."

Billy stared at his friends, feeling the fear come off them in waves. He was starting to become afraid himself.

"So, what're you gonna do . . . Owlboy?" Walter the firefly suddenly asked, a twisted sneer on his buggy face. The firefly had never liked Billy, believing that he'd been a lousy choice for the next Owlboy.

But standing there, looking at the giant bug and wishing that he had a giant boot to crush him flat, Billy had to ask himself . . .

What am I going to do?

CHAPTER 7

"Knock it off, Walter," Archebold warned, grabbing hold of the large bug and trying to shove it back inside his tuxedo coat pocket. "Things are bad enough without you causing trouble."

"No," Billy suddenly spoke up. "No, he's right. What *am* I gonna do about this?"

The bug chuckled as Archebold pushed him into the pocket.

"Don't listen to him, Billy," Archebold said. "He's just jealous because he can never be Owlboy."

"That's a lie!" Walter buzzed from deep within the goblin's pocket.

"Shush!" Archebold scolded, slapping the side of his jacket.

"No, I have to listen to him," Billy explained. "If I don't, everything he said to me when I first became Owlboy will end up being true. He didn't think I had what it takes to be a superhero, and now's my chance to prove him wrong."

"You don't have to prove anything to Walter," Halifax said. "He's just a bug whose butt glows."

Archebold came over and gripped Billy's arm. "It's really bad, Billy," the goblin said. "They waltzed right into the Roost as if they owned the place."

Billy was confused.

"They walked right in?" he asked. "How did they even know where it is?"

Archebold shrugged.

"It's almost as if they had inside information," Halifax whispered, looking around. "Like somebody told them exactly where to find it."

"That's not good," Billy said with a shake of his head.

"None of it's good, Bill," Archebold said. He started to walk around the garage.

"So this is where you live?" Halifax asked, following the goblin. "I wouldn't mind a place like this."

"This is just the garage," Billy said. "My room's in the house over there." He pointed toward the window in the door.

"Swanky," Halifax complimented Billy with a nod.

"Whatever," Billy said. "So what're we gonna do about Monstros, guys? Help me out here."

Halifax hovered around a plastic tub. "What's in here?" he asked.

"Stuff for my science project at school," Billy explained.

"Good gravy, Marie!" Halifax screamed, looking in the plastic crate. "There's enough heavy ordnance in here to wipe out an army!"

"Heavy ordnance?" Billy asked, joining the troll and Archebold at the tub. "It's just odds and ends I picked up at the store."

"Do they teach death in your science class, Billy?" Halifax asked. He reached inside the box and carefully removed two objects.

"Yeah," Billy said. "Those are potatoes. . . . What're you gonna do, bonk me in the head with them?"

"The potato has been outlawed in Monstros since pretty much the beginning. There's way too much power stored in one of these tubers."

The troll carefully set the potatoes down, as if afraid they might explode, and rummaged through the box. "I'm terrified by the destructive potential I see in here," he said, lifting up a bottle of vinegar and a box of baking soda.

"Those are for my volcano," Billy said. "It makes it erupt." He demonstrated with his hands.

"You could very well destroy the world if you're not careful," the troll warned, again looking down into the box. "You do know what you're doing, right?"

"Sure I do," Billy said. "But you've got to remember, things don't work the same here as they do in Monstros. This stuff is pretty harmless."

Halifax stepped back from the box. "Harmless? I just can't see it," he said, shaking his head.

And then Billy got an idea. "Hey, if these things are so destructive in Monstros, maybe we can use them to defeat the bad guys!"

Archebold stroked his chin. "In theory, that might be a good idea, but there are more of them than us," he fearfully explained. "It's like sending the Ghoul Scouts against the Monstros City Defense Corps."

"The Ghoul Scouts?" Billy asked.

"What, you don't have the Ghoul Scouts here?" Archebold asked, surprised.

Billy shook his head.

"Whatever," the goblin stated. "Even with the heavy-duty weapons, there just aren't enough of us."

The gears were starting to turn inside Billy's head; all those years of reading comic books finally paying off. This was just the kind of situation he'd read about thousands of times—the time for heroes to unite their incredible powers for the greater good.

It was time to form a superhero team.

The Fabulous Family of Five had come together to defeat X'Tros the Engorged. The Y-Guys had been close to defeat at the hands of their individual enemies until they'd joined together to form an amazing team of heroes. The Furious Furies had joined forces to kick butt because they were so furious all the time they needed to beat up bad guys to keep from beating up each other.

This was it. "What if we put together a team?" Billy suggested, his eyes twinkling excitedly.

"A team?" three voices responded.

"Yeah, a team of superheroes to fight a team of supervillains."

"Oh my," Archebold said. "We know there's you, but where would we get the other heroes?"

"OwlLad," Billy said, pointing at Archebold. The goblin gasped.

"The Hooter." Billy pointed at Halifax.

Then, as if on cue, the door to the garage banged open, revealing a strange figure standing in the doorway.

They all screamed, not sure who had chosen to interrupt this momentous occasion. Billy silently prayed that it wasn't one of his parents, because really, how would he explain a troll, a goblin and a giant firefly in the garage?

"What's goin' on in here?" the figure asked, stamping her foot.

And then Billy knew exactly who it was.

It must have been destiny.

"And Destructo Lass," Billy said pointing to his five-year-old neighbor, Victoria, who was standing in the doorway, hands on her hips. She was dressed rather strangely, wearing a ballerina skirt, tights, her winter jacket and cowboy boots.

"I'm not Destructo Lass, I'm a ballerina!" she bellowed, her tiny fist clenched in rage.

"How do you feel about Destructo Ballerina?" Billy asked, and watched as a smile slowly formed on the five-year-old's face.

His team was coming together.

His Flock of Fury.

"You're so dumb, when they ask your name you get stuck on the answer," the bite of heckleberry pie on the end of Klot's fork heckled as he shoved it in his mouth and began to chew.

"Mmmmmmmmmmmmmmm," the Monarch's red-skinned lackey moaned as he prepared for another bite of the insulting pie.

"Is that your face or are you minding it for a pile of maggots?"

"I don't think I've ever tasted heckleberry pie this fresh," he said, jabbing at the pie and shoveling bite after bite into his mouth.

Mukus was equally impressed with the cockroach cluster cookies and the deep-fried cephalopod on a stick. He held one in each hand as he and Klot made their way from the snack room to the monitor room, where they had left the Monarch.

"Hey," Klot said, coming to a stop. "Maybe we should have brought the boss back a piece of pie, or at least something bubbly to drink?"

Mukus thought about that for a moment, taking bites from his insect-filled cookie, then pulling a batter-covered cephalopod from its stick with his slime-covered teeth. "I think we should just ask him if we can get him anything. That way we get a chance to go back and get ourselves some more treats."

"I like the way you think," Klot said, breaking off another piece of pie. *"If ugly were a crime you'd get a life sentence,"* the piece of pie said as Klot brought it up to his mouth.

Still gnawing on the various treats, the lackeys entered the elevator and took it up to the monitor room.

"You have such a striking face," the last bite of heckleberry pie said.

Gulp!

"That stinks," Mukus said, pieces of cockroach spraying from his mouth.

"What does?" Klot asked.

"I didn't hear the rest of the heckle," the monster said. "Sounded like a good one."

Klot smiled. "Oh, I'm sure it would have been especially nasty," he said.

Mukus reached into the pocket of his jacket and removed a worm-covered pastry.

"Maggot muffin?" he asked.

"Certainly," Klot said, licking his lips and reaching for the still-squirming desert.

Mukus had removed another worm-covered treat and was about to take a bite when they heard a voice from the monitor room up ahead.

"Who's that?" Klot asked midbite, maggots squirming on his lips.

"I don't know," Mukus answered. "Maybe the boss has company."

They inched closer to the end of the hall and carefully peered around the corner.

The Monarch sat slumped in a chair before the multiple screens. "I . . . I used to love to watch these screens," he said softly, sadly, to himself. "For hours I would look for danger . . . danger to the city I . . . I . . ."

"Who's he talking to?" Mukus asked in a whisper.

"Himself, I think," Klot answered. "What gets me is what he's talking about. He's never watched those screens before."

"You're right," Mukus said, shoving the whole bug-covered muffin into his mouth. "For that to be true he would've had to have been here before, and that's just crazy . . . isn't it?"

A maggot crawled up Klot's nose and the monster began to sneeze insanely.

The Monarch was startled, sitting up in his chair. "Who dares creep up on me in my moment of contemplation?" he asked, his voice back to its more evil, world-conquering tone.

"It . . . it's just us, boss," Mukus said, dragging a choking Klot out into the open with him.

Klot massaged his throat, trying to get the squirming maggot to either go down the hatch to his belly or shoot from his mouth.

"Oh, it's you two." The Monarch reclined into his seat and returned his gaze to the screens. "You're lucky, I almost disassembled your atoms with a wave of my hand."

Klot suddenly coughed, sending a particularly large maggot flying through the air to land, wet and squirming, at the Monarch's feet.

"Glad you didn't disassemble us, boss," the blood-colored monster said. "We appreciate it."

The Monarch was silent.

"Is everything all right, boss?" Mukus worked up the courage to ask.

"I'm fine. Times such as this," the crime lord said, "when victory over my enemies is so close I can taste it . . . my head becomes filled with the strangest thoughts."

Again he seemed mesmerized by the images being broadcast from all over Monstros.

"Are you sure?" Klot demanded.

The Monarch brought his foot down upon the squirming maggot, crushing it with a juicy pop.

"I'm fine."

The Friday-night movie had done its trick, sending Billy's parents deep into dreamland. His father was snoring so loudly that he sounded like a chain saw going to town on a redwood.

Billy had snuck into the house, grabbed his costume from the book bag in his closet and headed back out to the garage without anybody being the wiser.

"We should get ready to haul this stuff over to the mausoleum," Billy said, looking around the garage. He found a wheeled suitcase, unzipped it and began to load the science fair stuff inside.

"Be careful with those!" Halifax screamed, running for cover as Billy picked up the potatoes.

Victoria giggled like a crazy person, picking up a potato of her own and chasing Halifax around the garage with it.

"We can't use the mausoleum entrance," Archebold said, helping Billy load the suitcase.

"Why not?" Billy asked. "Didn't you guys get here that way?"

The goblin shook his head. "No, we were ambushed on the shadow paths by the Sassafrases, and they blew up the stairway pretty good. It might be all right, but I'm not sure if it—"

Something crashed in the background behind them, and Billy flinched. Victoria was giggling all the louder now, and he didn't want to look.

"So how did you get here?"

Archebold pointed to where Billy had found them. "We used one of the unmapped paths."

"Unmapped?" Billy echoed.

A breathless Halifax joined them, glancing over his shoulder to make sure he wasn't about to be attacked with a potato.

"Sure," the troll said. "Did you think the only way to get from Monstros to Earth was in the Sprylock mausoleum?"

123

"Well, kinda," Billy said with a shrug.

"There are passages in the darkness of Monstros that can take you all over the world," Archebold chimed in.

"We were wicked lucky to find one to your garage," Halifax added.

"Wicked lucky to have a firefly with an awesome sense of direction with you," Walter added from his perch atop the handlebars of an old bike.

"Yeah, there was that," the troll conceded.

"*Yaaarrrrgh!*" Victoria screamed, shoving the potato into Halifax's face.

The troll promptly fainted and Victoria laughed so hard that she doubled over.

"I'm gonna pee," she screeched between bouts of hysteria.

"Don't you dare!" Billy warned, moving her across the garage. "You've got to get ahold of yourself if you're gonna help me with the bad guys," he told her.

"You sure she's a good idea?" Archebold asked, helping a moaning Halifax up. "Are we forgetting her last visit to Monstros, when she was used as a tool of destruction by the bad guys? She made an awful mess."

"I know," Billy agreed as Victoria started to calm down. "But I think her powers will come in really handy."

"Did you see him fall down, Billy?" Victoria giggled. "I showed him the potato and he went like this." She pretended she was Halifax and crashed to the floor, where she rolled around, laughing crazily.

"Nice," Halifax grumbled. "You humans are all twisted."

After a few moments, they finally got Victoria calmed down; then they were ready to leave.

"So you're saying there's a magical passage of shadow in a corner of my garage that will take us to Monstros? Who'da thunk it?" Billy said as he finished getting into costume.

Archebold had gone over to the corner and was moving some boxes out of the way.

"Well, you had a passage here a little while ago. Let's hope it's still here."

"The passage can disappear?" Victoria asked.

"That's one of the things that makes traveling the unmapped paths so tricky. They can change"—the goblin snapped his chubby fingers—"just like that."

"Just like that," Victoria repeated, trying unsuccessfully to snap her fingers.

"I got it, thanks," Billy said dryly.

Archebold plucked Walter from his shoulder. The giant firefly illuminated the floor of the garage, and Billy saw something that looked like a manhole.

"Looks like we're still good," Archebold said.

"Wow, would you look at that?" Billy said, pulling the wheeled suitcase over.

"You expect me to go down there?" Victoria asked.

"If you want to be part of the superhero team, you have to," Billy told her.

"Maybe I need to go home and get Mr. Flops," she said, making reference to her favorite stuffed animal, who strangely came to life in Monstros City.

"We don't have enough time, Destructo Ballerina," Billy said. "We have to go right now if we want to save the folks in Monstros from the bad guys."

Victoria thought about it for a second or two, watching as Walter flew down into the hole, lighting it up and making it not so scary.

Archebold and Halifax followed the firefly.

"Are you coming?" Billy asked her.

"Flops is gonna be very sad that he missed out," she said, sitting down at the edge of the hole and letting her legs dangle before jumping down.

Billy wished he could have helped Flops out. He would have gladly let the stuffed rabbit take his place on the journey back to the city of monsters.

A city under siege.

The unmapped shadow paths were cramped and cold and smelled like stinky cheese.

Walter flew a bit ahead of the team, his glowing

posterior providing them with enough light to see where they were going. The special night-vision mechanisms built into Billy's goggles helped him to see where they had been.

"Any idea how close we are?" he asked, stopping to pull on the ends of his gloves for a tighter fit before taking hold of the suitcase handle again.

Walter stopped too, hovering in the air before them.

"We're close, but I'm not sure how close," the insect buzzed. "That's the problem with the uncharted stuff—it's completely unpredictable. We could end up crawling out of a patch of shadow into somebody's living room."

"Would they have cake?" Victoria asked, eyes twinkling with the thought.

"What?" Billy asked. "Would who have cake?"

"The people whose living room we're going to, stupid head," she responded with an eye roll. "They have good cake in Monstros City."

The last time Victoria had been in Monstros, she had sampled their rather unusual treats before nearly bringing the city down around their ears. Billy thought it was funny that after all she'd gone through there, cake was the only thing she could think about.

"We don't even know if we're gonna end up in

somebody's living room," Billy explained. "So I wouldn't get my hopes up if I were you."

The little girl stamped her foot, and the resulting shock wave caused the shadow passage to wiggle and bend.

"Don't do that!" Archebold screeched. "These passages are extremely unstable. They can collapse around us and bury us in solid shadow."

"And without the proper tools we'd be sunk," Halifax added. "Ain't nothing more unpleasant than trying to tunnel out of shadow rubble."

Victoria put her hands over her ears. "Stop yelling at me!" she hollered. "All I wanted was some cake!"

"Knock it off," Billy warned, wagging his finger in front of her face. "Do you want to get us killed before we even go up against the bad guys? You've got to remember that the closer we get to Monstros, the more powerful your Destructo powers become."

She folded her arms across her chest and scowled.

"You didn't take a nap today, did you?" Billy asked.

"I hate naps," Victoria growled.

"Shhhhhhhhh!" Walter suddenly buzzed.

"Don't shush me, you big glow-butted bug," she snapped.

"Nice," Walter answered. "And I wasn't shushing you, I was shushing all of us. I think when you caused that little ruckus with the foot stomp, you somehow moved us closer to an entrance to Monstros."

The firefly flew down the passage for a better look.

"See, I might've helped us," she said, and stuck out her tongue.

"You still need a nap," Billy muttered beneath his breath, not wanting to get into it with a five-year-old. "For about a month." He dragged his suitcase down the shadow passage to join the others.

Billy wondered briefly why he had put himself through this by inviting Victoria along, but then he remembered the enormous power she had shown on her last visit to the city of monsters.

"Well?" Billy asked, stopping beside Archebold and Halifax.

Walter was buzzing around what looked to be a puckered hole in the wall of the tunnel. The firefly waved some of the air leaking from the hole toward his face. "Oh yeah," he said, his insect eyes closed as he inhaled the breeze. "That's Monstros, all right. Nothing smells like that."

Billy stepped closer to give the hole a look. "Seems kind of small."

"It'll stretch," Halifax said, reaching over and grabbing the hole on either side to pull it apart. "Shadow is very pliable."

"More tunnels!" Victoria complained, having caught up to them.

Billy felt his friends' disapproving eyes upon him. She was starting to drive them nuts, and who could blame them? Victoria was a pest with a capital *P*.

"Yep, more tunnels," Billy said. "And who knows, maybe there's cake on the other side."

"Cake?" she echoed, a disturbing smile spreading across her cherubic features.

"You never know," Billy said. "We could end up in a snack warehouse or something."

"Wow," she said, licking her lips. "Who's going first?"

"We should let Walter go first, then Archebold and Halifax, and then you can go. I'll be right behind you."

Victoria agreed, and things proceeded just as Billy had described. Billy imagined he was a piece of food passing through a large intestine. It was even colder and smellier inside this tunnel, and he couldn't wait to get out.

The passage suddenly angled upward, growing more spacious, and soon they didn't need to crawl anymore. A few minutes later, they were standing in an open pocket of shadow.

"Are we in Monstros yet?" Billy asked, righting his wheeled suitcase.

"Almost," Walter said, buzzing around a particular

section of wall. "Where we want to be is on the other side of this."

"Isn't there an exit?" Billy asked, confused. "Any way to get through the wall?"

"Remember, these are uncharted territories, Bill," Archebold explained. "The undiscovered country and all that gobbledygook." The goblin placed his hands on the wall and pushed. The darkness gave way as if made of rubber.

"Oh yeah, that's thin enough. We can cut our way through."

"Cut our way through?" Billy asked.

"And then will there be cake?" Victoria asked, doing a crazy little dance.

"Cake?" Halifax asked.

"Never mind her," Billy said. "We're going to cut through the shadow to get out?"

Halifax fished in one of the deep pockets of his overalls.

"Ahh! Here it is," the troll said, removing a small pocketknife and holding it out for Billy to see. "It's got a special shadow blade for cutting this stuff." He found the blade and snapped it into place.

Billy wasn't impressed. He'd seen bigger knives as accessories to some of his action figures, but he didn't say anything.

Halifax approached the wall and pushed on it a few

times, searching for the thinnest point, Billy guessed. Leaning in very close, the troll stuck the knife into the solid darkness and began to cut downward. The tiny blade cut through the rubbery darkness like the Furious Furies' Captain Razor's claws cut through evil.

"There," Halifax said, proudly stepping back from the entrance he'd cut and putting away his blade. "That should get us through all right."

"Get us through for cake!" Victoria cried, running toward the hole.

Billy reached out and grabbed her by the hood of her winter jacket. She kept running in place, hands extended, reaching for the darkness.

"Boy, she really loves cake," Archebold said. "But what if there isn't any—"

"I'll take care of it," Billy quickly interrupted the goblin. "You guys go ahead and I'll deal with that here."

Walter flew through the newly cut passage, followed by Archebold and Halifax.

"They're going, Billy," Victoria whined. "They're gonna get all the cake!"

Billy took her by the shoulders and spun her around.

"Victoria, I want you to listen to me," he said in his very serious voice. "There might not be any cake on the other side of that passage."

The little girl stopped struggling and stared into his goggles.

"No cake?" she asked in a teeny-tiny voice.

Billy shook his head.

"You promised!" she bellowed at the top of her lungs, the force of the words tossing him backward against the wall.

"Remember what we said about losing your temper here," Billy warned, picking himself up.

"I think you're lying," she said, arms folded. "I think you guys just want to get the biggest pieces and leave none for me."

"Victoria, I told you, there's no cake," he tried to explain. "I don't even know where the idea came from. It's something your crazy five-year-old brain made up."

"You're a crazy five-year-old brain!" she screamed, spinning around and running for the passage. "Nobody's gonna take my cake."

"Victoria, wait!" Billy cried, grabbing his suitcase and chasing after her.

The new passage was dark, but through the lenses of his goggles he could make out Victoria's shape running toward an exit not far away.

"Hey, wait up!" he yelled, his voice coming back at him in a warbly echo.

Billy was running as fast as he could, dragging the

suitcase behind him. He reached the exit, ducked his head and plowed through to the other side, ready to read Victoria the riot act for running off on her own—but then he stopped short.

Halifax, Archebold, with Walter perched on his shoulder, and Victoria were all standing perfectly still in front of him. Halifax had one of his hands clamped over Victoria's mouth.

"What's goin—" Billy began.

"*Shhhhhhhhhhhhhhhhhhhhhhhhhhhhhhhhhhhhhh!*" they all shushed in unison, spraying his face with a sheen of spit.

Billy wiped his goggles and saw Archebold pointing at something.

At first he thought it was a gigantic pile of dirty clothes, but then he noticed that it was moving . . . and snoring loudly.

What the . . . ?

Billy left his suitcase and crept over to inspect the snoring pile.

He almost choked on his tongue when he realized what it was. It was the Sassafras Siblings and their mother, lying on top of each other in a gigantic pile of snoring evil, weapons cradled lovingly in their arms.

Archebold had told Billy that the bad guys' leader had sent the siblings and their mother into the shadow paths to keep him from getting back to Monstros. He guessed they must have gotten tired of waiting and crashed for a quick nap.

Slowly and carefully, Billy backed up, returning to his friends.

"Of all the places we could've ended up, we land here in front of these guys?" Billy asked his friends in a whisper.

"Just call us lucky," Archebold whispered back with a shrug.

The Sassafras mound continued to snore, and Billy's brain immediately went to work trying to figure out what they should do next.

What did happen next was a bit of a nightmare.

Victoria had begun to struggle, trying to peel Halifax's dirty hand away from her mouth, when he leaned close to her ear and whispered, "See, even the Sassafrases need to take naps."

Halifax then let out an earsplitting scream as Victoria bit down on one of his chubby troll fingers as if it were an Italian sausage. He quickly pulled his hand away, trying to shake out the pain as Victoria placed her little hands on her hips and glared at them all.

"I'm not a little baby and I don't like stupid naps," she bellowed, stamping her foot and sending a powerful shock wave through the corridor of shadow.

And waking up the Sassafrases.

"Huzzah wah?" Mother Sassafras grumbled, lifting

her large head and peering around the chamber as she smacked her gigantic lips.

"But I don't want to go to school," Sigmund Sassafras whined sleepily. "And besides, I burned it down the other day."

"Mister Shooty?" Sireena said sleepily, sitting up. "Where's Mister Shooty?"

Billy guessed that she was looking for her gun, which had slid from her rather full lap onto the floor of the shadow passage. Hoping she would fall asleep again, he zipped over to get it for her. It weighed a ton, but he managed to place it on her lap, where her clawed hands finally found it.

"There you are, Mister Shooty," she said dreamily, eyes barely open. She lovingly petted the hard, angled metal.

Billy slowly, carefully, quietly returned to his friends, who were frozen in place. If they played their cards right, maybe the loathsome trolls would fall back asleep and they could get the heck out of there without being noticed.

But that would've been way too easy.

"Are those the guys with the cake?" Victoria asked, pointing to the mound of trolls.

Billy slapped his hand to his brow as Mother Sassafras came fully awake.

"Cake?" she exclaimed, her large eyes bulging with

interest. "I'll have just a little slice; I'm trying to watch my figure."

"Cake?" Sigmund yelped, immediately sitting up. "Is it my birthday already?"

"Not cake," Sireena growled, more awake than any of them. "More like dead meat."

"Outta the way!" Billy screamed, grabbing his friends and pushing them as the Sassafras sister suddenly grabbed Mister Shooty and began blasting away.

"That's not very nice!" Victoria scolded, climbing to her feet.

The trolls all had their weapons ready now, the whole Shooty family, and Billy thought he was going to have a heart attack.

"Nice?" Sireena smiled, looking down the barrel of her weapon at the five-year-old. "We killed nice a long time ago."

"I'm gonna enjoy blowing this one to bits," Sigmund chortled, aiming his weapon as well. "If it wasn't for her, we would have ended up as the kings of crime in Monstros."

Mother Sassafras pushed her children aside for a better look at Victoria. "Is this the horrible human child that caused my babies such problems?" she asked. "You nasty little thing. You had no right putting my precious children in the big house."

"Are we gonna turn her into a grease spot, or are we gonna talk her to death?" Sireena asked.

Billy saw his opportunity.

"Destructo Lass, use your powers now!" he screamed from the cover of shadows.

"I am *not* a Destructo Lass," Victoria yelled again, stamping her foot. "I'm a ballerina!"

The Sassafrases had just begun to shoot at the child as a new shock wave rocked the passage. Their shots went wild, completely missing the angry little girl.

"Hey," she said, turning back to them. "You could have shooted me."

"Hey, Victoria, if you're a ballerina, prove it," Billy called.

"What?" she asked, turning around to face him.

The Sassafras family was picking itself up off the floor and getting ready to fire their weapons again.

"I said, if you're a real ballerina, prove it!" Billy cried.

He had seen Victoria dance before, on occasions too numerous to mention, and to say that she had two left feet was being kind.

What was the word his father had used when he saw Victoria doing a dance number for her dolls in their driveway?

Spastic. Yeah, that was it.

Never one to ignore a challenge, and feeling as though she just might be the greatest dancer since

Angelina Ballerina, Victoria started one of her elaborate numbers.

"What's she doing?" Mother Sassafras demanded, stepping back just in case a piece of the child should fly off.

"I don't know," Sigmund whispered, his eyes locked on the little girl's movements.

"I think she's having a fit," Sireena said, obviously mesmerized.

Billy and the others could not help watching. He had never seen these moves before. The five-year-old squatted down almost to the floor with her hands above her head, then sprang into the air.

"Oh my," Archebold said.

"There's something really scary about this," Halifax added.

"I want to go back in your pocket now," Walter buzzed, crawling into one of Archebold's deep coat pockets.

Victoria was so lost in her dance that she wasn't paying a bit of attention to where she was going. Her movements became faster and faster as she got into the rhythm, moving across the corridor right at the Sassafrases.

"Look out!" Sigmund shrieked, attempting to get out of the little girl's way, but his mother blocked his path.

Victoria—eyes clamped shut in concentration—leapt, squatted and flung her arms out as she danced to a song that only she could hear.

"Kill it!" Sireena yelled, trying to aim her rifle. But the dancing child was too close and within seconds, Victoria—the Destructo Ballerina—was among them.

There wasn't a thing they could do to escape her Destructo Dance.

Tiny fists connected with flabby troll stomachs; feet, in the middle of kicks and leaps, pounded terrified troll faces and sent them flying.

She's a sight to behold, Billy thought as the Sassafrases were reduced to a moaning pile on the floor. *So much destructive power in one tiny body, it's sort of scary.*

Thank God she was on their side.

CHAPTER 8

It was almost time.

The Monarch sat before the flickering images of destruction that appeared on the multiple monitors inside the Roost, watching the devastation being wrought on the city of monsters by his villainous agents of doom.

I certainly made the right choices with this group, he thought, admiring the creativity they had brought to their attacks.

If they were not stopped soon, there would be no Monstros City left.

The Monarch moved closer to the edge of his seat, studying all the screens, attempting to look into the eyes of those who ran around the city in total panic.

He could see it there now, in their wide, terror-filled eyes. They wanted to be saved. They were desperate for a hero to make all the badness go away.

"It's time," the Monarch suddenly proclaimed, standing up from his seat.

Nearby, his lackeys—who had been filling their faces with snack foods—stood as well, wiping crumbs of fried cephalopod and insect-filled cookies from their faces.

"Time for what, boss?" Mukus asked eagerly. "Is it time for you to declare yourself ruler of Monstros City?"

"And to have everyone bow down to you as the grand supreme pooh-bah of evil and all-around swell guy?" Klot continued.

"No," the Monarch answered, again gazing at the scenes of chaos. "It's time to save it."

"Save it?" Mukus asked.

Klot laughed, sticking one of his red-clawed fingers in his ear and giving it a wiggle. "For a minute there, I could have sworn you said that it was time to save it, but we of course know how crazy that is and . . ."

The Monarch turned his hidden face toward them, nodding within his hood.

"For years I dreamed of being a hero," he said. "And I've worked very hard to finally create the conditions to make that dream come true."

The lackeys were holding each other, afraid.

"We . . . we don't understand," Klot said as Mukus nodded furiously, his dripping body sending spatters flying around them.

"What is there to understand?" the Monarch asked, spreading his arms wide.

"Monstros City needs a hero to replace the hated Owlboy, and I'm just that guy."

"This place looks kinda familiar," Billy said, slowly pushing open the door into what looked to be a storage room.

Archebold, Halifax and Victoria joined him as Walter buzzed above their heads, the light from his rear end illuminating the darkened room.

"Looks like we're in the back of a store," Halifax said, reading the writing on one of the boxes stacked in the corner. The box contained a product called Uncle Fred's Slugs in a Minute.

"I love Slugs in a Minute," Halifax said, licking his furry chops. "My mom used to make it for us on the nights she worked a double shift down at the filth factory."

"Filth factory?" Victoria asked, wrinkling her nose. "Sounds stinky."

Halifax nodded. "Yeah, a little. She was in charge of maintenance on the crud engines. Boy, she could make those babies sing. If it wasn't for my mom, a lot of monsters would have frozen their pimply behinds off in the chill season, I can tell you that."

"Fascinating," Walter hummed sarcastically as he checked out other parts of the room. "I can't wait to read the book."

Halifax looked as though he wanted to slowly rip the firefly's wings off, so before that could happen, Billy jumped in.

"I know I've been here before," he said, walking across the room. "I think there's a door right here."

It was there, just as he remembered.

"See?" he said, pointing it out to his teammates.

"I think this is the place where I ended up the first time I ever came to Monstros," Billy explained. "When I tried to give the Owlboy costume back and ended up falling into the stone crypt."

"Loser," Victoria chirped with a giggle.

Billy gave her the evil eye before turning the doorknob.

"I saved this little guy with a fireball for a head from these skeleton dudes that were trying to rob the store."

He pushed the door, but it stuck midway.

"Something's blocking it," Billy said, using his Owlboy strength to push harder and move the obstruction. "Oh wow." He gazed around. The store was in total disarray, all the shelving knocked over and product spilled on the floor. "It's totally wrecked."

Light fixtures hung loosely from the ceiling and sparks shot from exposed wire.

"This is what I was afraid of," Archebold said sadly as he passed through the doorway to join Billy in the store.

The others followed.

"What's that?" Billy asked.

"This is what bad guys do," the goblin said, picking up some of the shelving and trying to tidy things up a bit. "They wreck everything that's good."

Billy found himself suddenly becoming sad, with a truckload of angry right behind it.

"Who knows what else they've destroyed since we've been gone," Archebold added with a sigh.

Billy had heard enough. He hadn't been this angry since Randy Kulkowski had hung him from a coat hook by his underwear in third grade. The memory still made him wince, and he used the additional anger generated by the thought to move him to action.

Until he heard someone crying.

He was drawn to it, and climbed over the rubble,

trying not to step on anything that might still be use-able.

Billy found his old friend, the flame-headed guy, sitting on the curb in front of his wrecked store. The little guy was crying big tears of fire that dribbled down his chin and sizzled on the street.

Billy carefully approached, clearing his throat.

Slowly, the store owner turned to see who was behind him. "You!" he said, his dark eyes bulging with excitement. "It's really you!"

Normally Billy would have been flattered and kind of excited by the attention, but now, seeing what had happened to the guy's store, it just made him feel kind of depressed.

"Hey," Billy said with a little wave. "Remember me?"

"Remember you?" The monster rushed to Billy and threw his arms around the hero's waist. "How could I forget?" he said, giving Billy a big hug.

"Awww," Victoria said. "That guy's pretty cute."

The store owner's head was burning a dark, orangey color as he released Billy.

"I never believed a word of what they've been saying about you," he said, puffing his chest out proudly. Billy noticed that he was wearing a light blue shirt with a red apron on which the name SAMMY was stitched.

"Sammy, is it?" Billy asked.

Sammy nodded vigorously, sending sparks flying from his head like firewood snapping in a campfire.

"Who's been saying what about me?" Billy asked.

"The television and the newspapers," Sammy answered angrily. "They say you're incompetent . . . that you should have your superhero license revoked." The fire atop his round head was now burning bright red. "Do they have such a short memory?" he asked. "Do they not remember Zis-Boom-Bah and how you saved the city from a terrible fate?"

Billy smiled, a little embarrassed by Sammy's enthusiasm.

"Well, I did have a bad time the other night," he said, turning slightly to look at Archebold and Halifax, who were looking everywhere but at him.

"I said to my friend Zeeborg," Sammy continued, "I said, 'Zeeborg, Owlboy is just having a bad night. Don't you think that after all he's done he's entitled to one bad break?'"

"What did Zeeborg say?" Billy asked.

"He said they should take away your costume and make you run naked through the streets, but that's just Zeeborg. He's a very cranky monster."

"Oh," Billy said.

"I said to Zeeborg, 'You mark my words, when things turn very bad, we'll be begging for him to save us again.' " Sammy wagged his chubby finger at Billy and his friends. "And look," he said, spreading his arms and looking around at the deserted street. All of the stores looked as bad as Sammy's. "Look at what has befallen us."

"The bad guys?" Billy asked, feeling his fury on the rise again. He'd only been the hero of Monstros for a few months, but he found himself incredibly protective of it.

"It was like they had no fear," Sammy said sadly. "Like they knew we had chased you away."

Billy shook his head and placed a firm hand on Sammy's shoulder.

"You didn't chase me away," he said. "I would never leave Monstros unprotected."

"And that's exactly what I told Zeeborg," Sammy said, his flame now burning a cheery yellow.

The ground shook violently beneath their feet.

"What's that?" Sammy asked, his fire hair darkening with concern.

"Probably trouble," Billy said, making eye contact with his team. "Are we ready for this?"

They all turned toward the sound of destruction. Something was coming—something big, loud and heavy. It would be coming around the corner of Rigor onto Mortis Street at any second.

An old, beat-up truck, its back end loaded with

peeper fruit, flew down the street like a toy, the eyeball-like fruit rolling and spattering grossly on the ground.

"This is it," Billy said as the dark shadow of whatever it was blanketed the ground.

"I have to go to the bathroom," Victoria announced.

"Not now," Billy said as the threat appeared.

The robot was huge, its head a large, plastic bubble where whoever was controlling the mechanized instrument of destruction would have sat, but in this case there was more than one controller.

In fact, there were five.

The robot's head was filled with monkey demons—Slovakian Rot-Toothed Hopping Monkey Demons, to be precise. They all looked as though they wanted to be the one driving the metal monstrosity.

"Where the heck did they get that?" Billy yelled over the thunderous footfalls of the stomping robot. It was going out of its way to step on the cars parked along Mortis Street.

"My workshop," Halifax answered.

"Your workshop?" Billy asked. "Are you telling me you made that?"

The giant robot picked up speed, jogging toward them on enormous robotic feet.

"You know how it is," Halifax said, rolling on the ground to avoid being ground to a paste. "It was a rainy

Saturday afternoon, I had some spare parts left over from a lawn mower I had just fixed . . ."

"And you built a giant robot?" Billy asked, avoiding twin laser beams shot from a weapon that had suddenly emerged from the robot's barrel chest.

"I told you it was a bad idea," Archebold screeched, peeking out from behind a fire hydrant, a terrified Sammy beside him.

The blast struck a mailbox, blowing it up and sending the mail inside into the air like confetti.

"Happy New Year!" Victoria screamed as she threw her hands into the air.

The Bounder boys immediately noticed the little girl dancing in the snow of confetti and headed toward her.

Not wanting to explain to Mrs. McDevitt how her daughter was squished into something resembling a pancake, Billy ran toward the oblivious little girl.

"Victoria, look out!" he yelled, watching as the giant robot loomed above her, raising one of its legs, preparing to bring a foot down on her five-year-old head.

The foot descended, and he could hear the sounds of the Bounder boys screaming and laughing.

"A *giant robot?*" he imagined Victoria's mom shrieking, immediately taking a big gulp of the special grape juice she drank in moments of stress.

"A *giant robot driven by five Slovakian Rot-Toothed Hopping Monkey Demons, to be precise,*" he saw himself explaining.

There was sure to be more screaming and drinking of the special grape juice, and Billy knew that it was just way too much drama for him. He dug deep into a special reserve of strength and power that he had stored for occasions just like this, and for getting the last chocolate pudding at lunch before Danny Ashwell had the chance.

Billy was suddenly with Victoria beneath the enormous metal foot. The little girl was still lost in her own world, bent down picking up pieces of the shredded mail.

"This one looks like a butterfly," he heard her say as he lifted his arms, catching the falling foot in his hands.

Planting himself, he used all his Owlboy strength to hold the foot in place.

"Forget . . . the . . . butterfly," he grunted, the sound of the robot's mechanics whining and grinding as the Bounders did everything they could to finish the job.

Victoria stood up, turning toward him with a piece of jagged envelope in hand. "This one looks like an ocelot," she said, holding it up so that he could see.

Billy wasn't sure he'd ever done anything quite so hard. The Bounders were trying to kill them, and Billy was the only thing keeping him and Victoria from becoming giant red stains on the ground.

A piece of trash that looked like an ocelot wasn't really on his list of important concerns at the moment.

"I . . . don't even . . . know what . . . an ocelot . . . is . . . ," Billy moaned, pushing against the increasing pressure of the giant robot's foot.

"It looks like this," Victoria said, and reached up to shove the piece of paper right beneath his nose.

The Bounders must have done something while at the controls, diverting all power to the giant robot's leg, because suddenly Billy was no longer holding the foot back, and he felt it start to push him down.

"This one looks sort of like a baby chick," Victoria said, dropping the ocelot to pick up another piece of envelope.

"You know what a baby chick looks like, right?" she asked sarcastically.

For a minute, he thought about diving out from beneath the foot and letting it squash the preschooler, the explanation that he would owe the little girl's mother not seeming all that difficult anymore. But he decided that maybe letting one of his teammates—one of his Flock of Fury—get crushed might not look so good for him.

So instead of jumping out of danger's path, Billy converted his annoyance into raw power.

"I'll show you what a baby chick looks like!" Billy screamed in quite possibly one of the most bizarre super-heroic cries of exertion ever uttered. A burst of strength exploded from his body. He pushed the giant robot's foot so ferociousy the mechanized assassin flipped backward. The robot went tumbling into the street with such force that the clear domed head of the robot shattered on impact.

Billy dropped to his knees, totally exhausted and gasping for breath. He hadn't been this tired since reaching the level of Galactic Imperator on *Star Commando Thirteen* for ZBox 499.

"Peep! Peep! Peep!" Victoria said, making the piece of envelope she was still holding in her tiny hand dance in front of his face. "Victoria still has to go to the bathroom. . . . Peep! Peep! Peep!"

He didn't have the strength to do anything but kneel there and let the baby-chick-shaped piece of paper dance on his head.

"Are you all right?" Archebold asked as he ran to Billy's side. "That was absolutely amazing!"

"I wouldn't have believed it if I hadn't seen it with my own eyes," Halifax added.

"I knew you could do it," Sammy said, patting him on the back. "Those monkey demons didn't have a chance."

Billy was only half listening to his friends. He'd seen some movement near the toppled giant robot and was curious about what was going on.

The Bounder boys emerged from the damaged cockpit, bouncing on their spring-heeled shoes and looking ready for round two.

"He broke our robot," Benny grumbled, brushing pieces of glass from the front of his vest.

"I loved that robot," Bobby said, starting to cry.

"It was like another brother to me," Bernie added as he checked his springs to make sure nothing was stuck to them.

"I say we stomp Owlboy and his friends into the dirt in honor of our fallen mechanical brother," Balthasar proposed.

"Maybe we could stomp on them every year at this exact time and make it a holiday," Bailey suggested.

"Brilliant!" the monkey demons screeched all at the same time. Then they slowly began their bouncing approach.

Billy struggled to stand, his legs trembling as if they were rubber bands. He didn't know if he had any fight left in him.

"What are we gonna do, Billy?" Archebold asked.

"Peep! Peep!" Victoria was still playing with the paper, making it dance on Billy's head.

"We'd better think of something fast, because those monkeys are getting kind of close," Halifax said, backing away.

Billy considered throwing Victoria at the monkey demons and letting her drive them insane, but that was probably too slow a process. Just then, he heard the sound of voices behind him.

"Looks like you could use a hand," a voice commented.

They all turned to see four old goblins dressed in tight-fitting costumes that mimicked the color and style of his own.

"Grandpa Artemus?" Archebold asked. "Is that you?"

"Not at the moment, Archebold," the old goblin said, his hands on his hips. "Right now me and the fellas are in superhero mode."

Billy couldn't believe his eyes. It was like his prayers had been answered. Archebold's grandfather and his friends—Saul, Percy and Morty—had all been sidekicks to the last three Owlboys that had protected Monstros before Billy, and here they were—the newest members of his Flock of Fury arriving for duty. Even Morty, who was nothing but a cobweb and dustcovered goblin skeleton in a wheelchair, looked ready—*as much as that was possible*—to defend the city they loved.

"You said I should give you a ring if I ever needed a hand," Billy said with a relieved smile. "Looks like you saved me from having to make the call."

Realizing that the size of Billy's flock had just increased by four, the Bounders attacked with wild abandon. Before Billy could even begin to think about his plan of defense, the old goblins were already on the move.

"Let's show 'em how we dealt with punks like this in the old days," Artemus growled as he took hold of Morty's wheelchair. Saul and Percy jumped into Morty's bony lap, and Artemus wheeled them all toward the advancing monkey demons.

Billy immediately felt guilty for letting the old-timers be first into battle. He moved to join in when he felt a small hand grip his arm. It was Archebold.

"Let them try first," the little goblin said. "They've been waiting years to do something like this. It'll do wonders for their self-esteem."

The former sidekicks let out screeching war cries as the wheelchair carrying them crashed into the center of the bouncing monkey demons. Three of the Bounder boys managed to leap out of harm's way, but Bailey and Bernie didn't move quite fast enough and got their feet run over.

"My toes!" Bailey screamed, hopping up and down and letting out an earsplitting screech with each hop. "It hurts to hop!"

Bernie had dropped to the ground and removed his coiled boots. Pulling his feet up to his mouth, he blew on his red and swollen toes.

"Not fair," he cried. "Not fair at all. Don't these goblins know that our feet are our livelihood?"

"They don't care," Bailey answered, trying hard not to bounce. "All they care about is stopping the bad guys. . . . Well, bad guys have feelings too, you know!"

Artemus laughed, punching an old wrinkled fist into the palm of his other hand.

"I love it when they whine, eh, boys?" he asked his partners.

"Like little babies," Saul responded with a tough-guy snarl.

"Maybe we should call 'em the Bounder girls," Percy teased.

Cough! Morty added, a cloud of dust and cobwebs shooting from his skeletal mouth.

The remaining Bounders had bounced back and stood in front of their injured brethren.

"No need for name calling," Bobby Bounder cried indignantly.

"Sticks and stones may break our bones," Balthasar said. "And wheelchairs crashing into us, of course."

"And big rocks," Benny added. "Big rocks could break stuff, too."

All the monkey demons agreed.

"Enough of this chatter," Artemus yelled. "We're gonna give you boys—and I use the term loosely—a chance to surrender, but if you don't drop to your knees with your hands behind your monkey heads, things are gonna get real ugly."

"I don't believe it," Billy whispered to Archebold. It actually appeared as if the Bounder boys were considering Artemus' offer.

"Told you they were tough," Archebold said, a proud smile on his goblin features.

And that was when things went bad.

"That nasty monkey is getting away!" Victoria suddenly screamed as Bailey Bounder weakly hopped over to the wreckage of the giant robot.

"They're going for the robot!" Halifax warned.

The old goblins started to move on the Bounders but were driven back by the speed of the bouncing monkeys.

"We gotta help," Billy said, already on the go.

But it was too late. Bailey Bounder had emerged from the fallen robot wielding a double-barreled laser rifle.

"This is for my toes!" the monkey screamed, firing wildly.

The blasts were coming fast and furious, and the Flock scattered. Twin beams of scarlet destruction raced through the air, narrowly missing Billy before striking Sammy's store, causing it to explode.

"No!" the little flame-headed shopkeeper cried sadly. Archebold had to hold on to the guy to keep him from running into the burning building.

Billy had had just about enough of this nonsense.

His entire team was hiding, and the Bounder boys were laughing insanely as they gathered around their laser-wielding brother. Their giggles became louder and higher pitched with each new object Bailey destroyed.

Billy quickly looked around and spied the suitcase he'd dragged from his garage. He grabbed it and dove for cover behind a parked car.

"Get him!" Balthasar screamed. "It's Owlboy, he's the one we want!"

Bailey fired the lasers again, twin bolts of sizzling death looking to make Billy history. But they missed, which bought him enough time to do what he needed to.

As fast as he could, Billy unzipped the suitcase and flipped back the lid. Halifax had said that many of his projects would be considered quite dangerous in the world of monsters, and Billy was hoping to find one that would put the Bounder boys in their place.

He moved some stuff around, and beneath a box of baking soda and some stray pieces of paper covered with notes and drawings, he found exactly what he was looking for.

The potato crackled with a bluish energy. If he hadn't been wearing his special goggles, it would have been blinding.

"I guess Halifax was right," Billy said, carefully reaching down to pick up the energized vegetable. His entire body began to tingle.

The Bounders urged Bailey to fire again, and Billy looked up to see the Slovakian Rot-Toothed Hopping Monkey Demon aiming down the barrels of the weapon at him.

As Bailey fired, Billy hurled the potato at the Bounder boys with all his might. If it had been a dodge-ball throw, he was certain that it would have knocked at least two opponents from the game.

He had no idea what to expect from the potato.

The ground beneath his feet exploded into rubble as the twin laser beams struck, hurling him backward to the street. Billy managed to roll onto his stomach just in time to see the potato land, the bluish white energy intensifying.

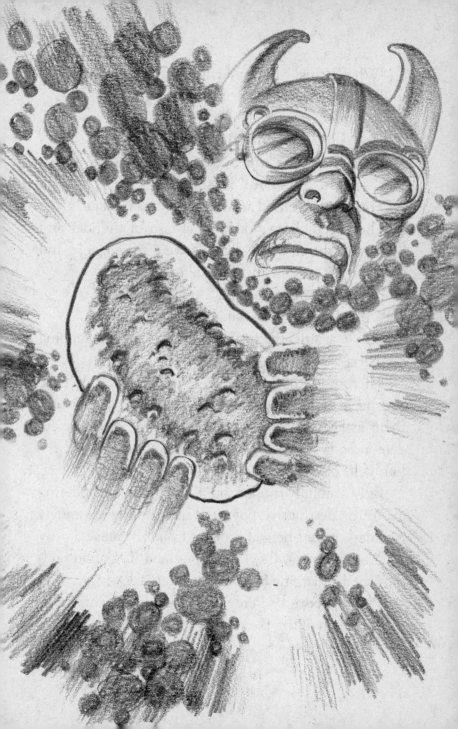

"What's this?" Balthasar asked, bouncing over to study the object.

"Looks like some kind of vegetable," Bobby answered.

"Looks like a potato," Benny said.

It was Balthasar who suddenly realized the danger they were in. "A potato!" he shrieked.

The others realized as well, but it was too late.

The vegetable exploded in a flash of thunder and light, and the monkey demons were tossed here and there with the intensity of the blast.

Billy just stared in awe.

"Told you they were dangerous," Halifax said.

"Do it again!" Victoria screamed happily, clapping her hands.

There was still one potato left, but Billy didn't see the need. The Bounders were bouncing away from them as fast as they could, the fur on their monkey-demon bodies standing on end as if charged with a zillion volts of static electricity.

Billy carefully zipped up the suitcase, wondering about the destructive potential of the other seemingly harmless objects he had brought from his garage.

"You did it, Owlboy!" Artemus and his goblin buddies cried, emerging from their hiding places.

"You better run!" Percy screamed, shaking his fist in the direction of the Bounders.

"You tell 'em, Percy," Saul said with a nearly tooth-less smile.

"No," Billy said in a loud voice, watching as the last of the monkey demons rounded the corner and disappeared.

The others all stopped, looking at him.

"I didn't do it," Billy said, shaking his head. "We all did it." He watched as proud smiles appeared on all their faces.

"The Flock of Fury did it."

"Is that what we're calling ourselves?" Artemus asked.

Billy nodded.

"I like it," the old goblin said, and his friends nodded in agreement. "It's got pizzazz."

Billy turned and noticed scared faces peeking out of broken windows and shattered doorways.

"It's all right," Billy called to them. "You're safe now."

One by one they emerged, the frightened citizens of Monstros, driven into hiding by attacks most heinous.

"I'm sorry," a yellow-skinned creature with tiny wings and a bulbous head said to him.

"For what?" Billy asked, confused.

"I'm sorry for having doubted you," the creature

confessed. "I believed that stuff that was in the news-papers and on the TV."

"I did too!" a fish with human legs said as he came out of his hiding place.

"Me too," said another resident that looked more like a ball of dust than an actual living thing.

They encircled Billy and his team, the apologies coming quickly now. Billy was just glad that they had regained their faith in him, and he was bound and determined that they would never lose it again.

Out of the corner of his eye he saw Sammy standing in front of his store, his flaming head—which now burned a sad, dark orange—bowed in sorrow.

Billy left the crowd.

"Hey," he said, standing beside Sammy.

The store owner glanced briefly at Billy before looking back to the store. "It's okay," he said.

"What is?" Billy asked, looking into the blackened remains.

"That my store got wrecked," Sammy explained. "You tried."

"Just not hard enough," Billy said.

Sammy looked back at him, shaking his round, burning head. "No, that's not true. You tried as hard as you could. These things happen, and I understand that."

Billy ran a gloved finger through the thick black

soot that covered the window frame. "How would you feel if we helped you rebuild your store?" he asked.

"Rebuild it?" Sammy asked, a gigantic smile threatening to split his moon-shaped face. The fire atop his head lightened to a vibrant yellow.

"Yeah, how would that be?"

"That would be amazing," Sammy answered.

Billy turned to his team.

"Hey, Halifax," he called out.

The troll turned.

"We're gonna help Sammy rebuild his store, all right?"

The troll gave him two big thumbs-up.

"Thank you, Owlboy," Sammy said, hugging Billy for a second time that night.

Billy felt his face begin to flush with embarrassment as he tried to pull away. "That's cool," he said. "Glad to help."

More citizens had emerged from hiding, and Billy was beginning to think that maybe they'd have a little while to catch their breath and put a better plan together. Then a centipede wearing a heavy, multisleeved sweater pointed down the street.

At first Billy thought it might be the Bounders coming back for seconds, but he soon realized that it was officers of the Monstrous City police force, led by their chief, the rock-bodied Chief Bloodwart.

Billy was psyched at the sight of the police officers . . . until he realized that they were running.

The Gaseous Ghost flew through the air behind the fleeing police officers, streams of noxious-smelling fumes streaming from his fingers. A short, armored shape that could only have been the villain Vomitor appeared next. The tiny creature opened its mouth extremely wide and a flood of spew gushed from his maw to sweep the police officers off their feet.

"On your toes, team," Billy announced, pointing to the scene unfolding before them. "This isn't over till the fat lady sings."

"What fat lady?" Victoria asked. "You know, that's not very nice, calling somebody fat. Where is she, anyway?"

Billy didn't have the chance to explain the figure of speech. Instead, he chose to run toward the police officers, who were now splashing around in the thick puddles of grossness that had come from Vomitor's mouth.

Billy turned to see if his team was following.

They stood just beyond the flow of vomit, watching him with expressions that said so many things:

I'm afraid.

Can I actually be a hero?

Am I too old for this?

I still have to go to the bathroom.

"Well?" he demanded. "Am I gonna be doing this alone?"

Without waiting for an answer, he turned back to the police officers, trying to help as many as he could to regain their footing in the foul-smelling, viscous ooze.

Chief Bloodwart was having a particularly hard time in the spew, so Billy went to help him.

"I've got you, Chief," he said, giving the rock cop enough leverage that he could get to his feet.

"Many thanks, Owlboy," the chief said. "To you, and to your people."

Billy slowly turned to see that, indeed, he wasn't alone. His Flock was there to back him up, helping the police officers, and anybody else that had been caught in the disgusting flood, reach safety. The old-timers were loading people onto Morty's wheelchair and pushing them out of harm's way. Archebold and Halifax had salvaged some parts from the fallen robot to create stilts that allowed them to wade through the muck and pluck the needy from the disgusting stomach juices. Even Victoria was doing her part, using the powers of her Destructo Touch by stomping her feet on the ground, causing cracks to appear and drain the vomit.

Billy smiled again, watching his team at work.

"How nice," a cackling voice mocked from above.

The Gaseous Ghost flew over their heads, his nasty

aroma making Billy want to gag. Vomitor's metallic face smiled as he surveyed the disgusting damage, and, as if things weren't bad enough, the Bounder boys were back, their fur still looking as though they'd rubbed their entire bodies with balloons.

"It would seriously touch my heart to see such unity," the Ghost said, flitting around in the sky above them. "Too bad I don't have one." He cackled insanely.

The vomit had been reduced to only a few stinking puddles, and Billy gestured for his team to join him.

"You and the boys might want to step back," Billy told Chief Bloodwart. "This could get ugly."

The Bounder boys had joined Vomitor and the Gaseous Ghost.

"What's that smell?" Balthasar asked, pinching his nose with his fingers.

Bailey pointed to the ghost above their heads.

"Ohhhhh," all the monkey demons said in unison, suddenly understanding.

Billy planted his feet and clenched his hands into fists. He was ready for this, ready to fight for Monstros . . . ready to fight for *his* city.

But were the others?

"Ready for this, guys?" he asked.

"I was born ready," Artemus said, cracking his knuckles.

"Beats the heck out of shuffleboard," Saul added.

Percy bent his neck one way with a crack, and then the other. "Hope I don't hurt these losers too bad."

Billy knew about the old-timers, but he wasn't sure about the others.

"How's about it, OwlLad? Hooter? Destructo Lass?"

"Destructo Ballerina!" Victoria screamed.

He was still waiting for their final answer when something in the sky began to roar.

What now? Billy thought with a roll of his eyes. He couldn't imagine the day getting any worse, but it kept right on surprising him.

He looked up into the sky to see something huge descending from the clouds.

"What the heck is that?" Archebold squawked as the whole team looked up.

"Looks like a giant robotic octopus," Halifax answered, staring up at the huge metallic vessel as it dropped from the clouds to the city skyline. "But I could be wrong."

Unfortunately, he wasn't.

Billy held his breath as he watched the eight-tentacled sky craft hover just above the city street behind the gathered villains.

"Something tells me we're pretty much outnumbered," Artemus said with a gulp.

The Gaseous Ghost cackled again, rubbing his green, smoky hands together in anticipation.

"This is going to be ugly," he said.

And as much as it pained him to admit it, Billy had to agree.

CHAPTER 9

"**W**here are your big words now, tough guys?" Vomitor gurgled over the disgusting sounds from his belly.

The Gaseous Ghost giggled insidiously. "Don't seem to like it too much when you're outgunned."

The Bounder boys were laughing like a pack of hyenas, as if they could sense the massacre to come and were being driven insane by the promise of blood.

Billy was seriously considering ordering his team to retreat. There was no way they could stand up to the Ghost, Vomitor, the Bounders *and* a giant mechanical octopus.

He couldn't even imagine the Furious Furies being able to pull victory out of this one.

The octocraft's huge metal tentacles writhed in the air, and Billy imagined them snatching up his teammates and squeezing the life from them like the last remnants of toothpaste from a tube.

"Now that the master is here, the fun can really begin," the Gaseous Ghost stated as wisps of nasty, eye-watering stink drifted from his outstretched fingertips.

The Ghost turned his vaporous head toward the octocraft.

"What do you say, boss?" the Ghost asked it. "Do we show these do-gooders how powerful it is to be bad?"

The mechanical octopus responded by lifting one of its mighty tentacles, and Billy found himself tensing for action.

Who knew what was going to happen next, but he and his team needed to be ready. He was about to tell his team to watch their backs when the unthinkable happened.

The octocraft's tentacle hovered over the head of the laughing ghost, and a small door slid open at its tip. The Ghost had just enough time to turn and look up into the opening, the beginnings of a question on his gaseous lips. "What the . . . ?"

The foul-smelling villain was suddenly sucked into the mechanical tentacle, the whine of its powerful motor reminding Billy of his mother's old vacuum cleaner.

The Ghost shrieked for about a second and was suddenly gone.

Billy wasn't quite sure what he had just seen, and neither were the other villains.

Archebold gazed at him quizzically.

"Don't ask me," Billy said, continuing to watch, curious to see what was going to happen next.

Vomitor suddenly turned around. "Hey," he grumbled. "What did you just do with—?"

Another of the tentacles whipped down to reveal a strange-looking device, and before the short, metal-clad villain with the perpetually upset stomach could even finish, it had zapped him with a flash of white.

Everybody had covered their eyes except Billy, whose special Owlgoggles shielded his vision.

The weirdness train kept right on rolling.

In front of them, Vomitor was now sealed in what looked to be a large plastic bubble.

Billy had once had a friend who used something similar for his hamster. He didn't think the hamster had liked it all that much, and he was sure that Vomitor didn't. The tiny armored monster roared within the bubble, his screams fogging up the inside of his plastic prison.

"That's a good idea," Halifax said, stroking his chin.

"Hope he don't, y'know . . . ," Victoria said, pretending to throw up.

Which is exactly what Vomitor did. The armored creature opened his mouth as wide as he could and began to spew inside the confines of the bubble. It didn't take more than a few seconds before the villain was swimming in a sea of his own bile.

The Bounders seemed to know what was up, but they didn't move fast enough.

One by one, the Slovakian Rot-Toothed Hopping Monkey Demons became snagged in beams of yellow energy streaming from the tips of the octocraft's eight appendages.

Billy was flabbergasted to see that the beam of energy had somehow rendered the Bounder boys weightless, leaving the demon monkeys floating helplessly in the air like feathers caught in a draft.

"Help us!" Balthasar screamed, trying desperately to keep from spinning end over end. "That's what you hero guys are supposed to do, right?"

"I want a monkey balloon!" Victoria demanded, pulling on Billy's sleeve. "Get me a monkey balloon!"

All Billy could do was stare at the current state of the villains that, mere minutes ago, had been set to kick the Flock's butts royally: the Gaseous Ghost sucked away someplace; Vomitor trapped in a bubble of his own spew; and the Bounder boys weightless, unable to hop or bounce on anything.

If he didn't know better, he'd think that whoever was inside that metal octopus was trying to help the good guys.

But that's completely bonkers, isn't it?

The air was suddenly filled with the sound of trumpets, as if royalty was about to appear. The music was coming from the octocraft, and Billy couldn't wait to see what was going to happen next.

A doorway appeared in the front of the craft, and a platform, which looked sort of like the octopus's tongue, extended from the body of the mechanical beast.

"What now?" Archebold muttered as two shapes moved down the platform toward them.

Billy wasn't sure who they were, but they certainly didn't look like anything special. One had leathery bright red skin. The other looked as though he was sculpted from slime.

They were both very serious.

Standing at attention on either side of the metal platform, the pair waited for the trumpeting to stop, and when it did, the one with the red skin cleared his throat.

"May I now present to you, the one, true superhero of Monstros City!" the leathery monster proclaimed at the top of his lungs.

One true superhero? What the heck is going on? Billy wondered.

The Flock looked at each other in confusion as a muttering buzz spread through the crowd of citizens behind them.

It was the slimy one's turn next.

"Put your paws, claws, hands and tentacles together for . . . the Monarch of Monstros City!"

And a figure clad in a long, flowing robe of bright red, his features hidden by a hood, emerged from the craft and slowly descended the platform.

Billy had a very bad feeling about this.

"As my two colorful compatriots have just mentioned, I am the Monarch," the hooded figure announced with a bow.

The two creatures on either side of the platform began to clap wildly, the slimy one whistling through his fingers and sending trails of yuck sailing through the air.

"And, as you can see, I have arrived just in time to save the day," the Monarch finished.

Billy wasn't sure what to make of the situation. He guessed he should thank the Monarch for the help.

"Thanks a lot for the hand with those bad guys," he said, stepping forward. "We really appreciate it."

Billy couldn't see within the darkness of the Monarch's hood, but he knew that the mysterious figure was staring at him. He could feel it, like hot needles poking into his face.

"I only did what you and yours could not," the Monarch announced. "Another indication that you and your ilk will no longer be required in Monstros."

Billy stumbled back as if pushed.

"No longer required?" he repeated. "What the heck is that supposed to mean?"

"I would think it obvious," the Monarch said with a low, rumbling chuckle. "Monstros has a far more effective champion to protect them from villainy now."

"Yeah, and who's that supposed to be, stupid face?" Victoria yelled, pushing past Billy to confront the supposed hero.

"Maybe if most of the city's crimes were occurring at the local day care," the Monarch replied. "But alas . . ."

He waved his black-gloved hand in the air with a flourish.

Billy grabbed Victoria by the shoulder and pulled her back.

"Any idea who this guy is?" Billy asked Chief Bloodwart, who was standing beside him, out of the corner of his mouth.

"There's kind of an urban legend about this extremely powerful criminal mastermind known as the Monarch," he told Billy. "He's supposedly behind all the crime that goes on in Monstros, but I always figured it was just a myth."

"Well, if that's who this is, he thinks he's a good guy now," Billy pointed out.

"A good guy," the Monarch repeated, slowly bringing his gloved hands together. "I always dreamed about being a good guy . . . a hero for the city that I love . . . and now it has at last come true."

Artemus, pushing Morty's chair, stepped forward along with Percy and Saul.

"And we say welcome to the club," the old goblin said. "If there's one thing there's plenty of room for, it's heroes."

The Monarch closed his hands into fists.

"No," he declared, shaking those fists in the air. "There can be only one true hero for Monstros City, and that is me."

"Let me see what I can do," Billy said to the old goblins, hoping he could defuse a potentially explosive situation.

"There's something about that one's voice," Artemus said to him, stroking his ancient chin as he glared at the Monarch. "Something familiar."

"Do you think you know who he is?" Billy asked the goblin.

"Give me a minute," Artemus said. "I'm sure it'll come to me."

Billy cheerfully addressed the Monarch: "What my friends are trying to say is that we have no problem if you want to be a hero in Monstros. There's plenty of crime for everybody to fight . . . more villains than you can shake a stick at . . . bad guys up the wazoo, so to speak." He laughed nervously, not sure he was getting through to the hooded figure.

"*I must be the only one!*" the Monarch bellowed at the top of his lungs. He then shot out his arm, a strange gunlike device appearing in his gloved hand.

Billy prepared to leap out of the way but wasn't fast enough. A beam of pulsing light struck him, engulfing his entire body. He was stunned to find that he could no longer move.

"Look at you," the Monarch scoffed. "Helpless as a kitten."

"Don't forget," Billy said, struggling to no avail to free himself from the effects of the paralysis ray. "Kittens have some pretty nasty claws . . . and they can bite, too!"

The Monarch adjusted a knob on his paralysis ray and Billy suddenly floated up into the air.

"Me next!" Victoria cried, jumping up and down.

Archebold tried to grab Billy's hand as he rose above them, but missed.

Who is this Monarch guy? Billy wondered as he hovered above the street like a Macy's Thanksgiving Day Parade balloon.

"Can't we talk this out?" he asked aloud, trying to

maintain some modicum of dignity as he spun in the air. "We're heroes, you're a hero, so why don't we just—"

"I'm the hero," the Monarch boasted. "The one and only."

"Don't you think that's . . . you know, a little greedy?"

"Silence!" the Monarch demanded. "We'll let the city decide."

Billy found himself floating higher now, drifting over the crowd of citizens that had gathered on Mortis Street.

"Citizens of Monstros City," the Monarch's voice boomed. "I ask you . . . is this the pathetic and weak kind of hero that you want protecting you from evil?"

Billy was spinning around really fast now, and he thought he just might hurl. *Great*, he thought. *That'll help them decide.*

He tried to focus on the crowd below. The number of citizens had grown quite a bit, and he could see his Flock of Fury waiting as well. At least he'd get some votes in his favor.

"I ask you again," the Monarch said. "Is this the sad kind of hero you want protecting you from harm?"

And the citizens of Monstros answered.

"Yes!" they all cried as one.

"Excuse me?" the Monarch asked, laughing nervously.

"I must have misheard you, so I'll ask the question again. People of this great city, is this the kind of hero that—?"

"Yes!" they answered again, not even giving the mysterious hooded figure the chance to finish his question.

The Monarch twisted something on the device in his hand. Instantly, Billy found himself dropping to the street below.

"Hup! Hup!" He watched as Artemus pushed Morty's wheelchair beneath him just in time to cushion his fall.

"Thanks, guys," Billy said, climbing off the skeleton.

"Don't mention it," Artemus said.

A cloud of dust exploded from Morty's mouth.

"So be it!" the Monarch was yelling. "If you don't want me as your hero and savior, then I guess you won't mind if I put things back the way they were before I arrived!"

From within the sleeves of his robe, the Monarch produced another device that reminded Billy of one of those fancy universal remotes that he'd seen down at the Big Buy store. The hooded figure punched some buttons on the device while pointing it at the villains that had been put on ice.

"Not good," Billy said, guessing what was about to happen.

One of the octocraft's tentacles rose, the tip of the limb flipping back to allow a nasty-smelling green cloud to escape—the Gaseous Ghost. The bubble surrounding Vomitor vanished with a loud pop, releasing a stream of spew as well as the squat, armored villain. And finally, the Bounder boys were given back their gravity. The Slovakian Rot-Toothed Hopping Monkey Demons dropped to the street, where they eagerly bounced, happy to have weight and heft again.

"If you won't accept me as your hero," the Monarch announced, "then maybe you'll like me better as a villain."

The hooded figure paused before raising him arms.

"Let's continue where we left off, shall we?" he growled. "Let's tear Monstros City down around these do-gooders' ears! Attack!" the Monarch screamed raggedly, commanding the released villains into destructive action.

Billy was ready, and as he glanced over at the others, he saw that they too appeared prepared for what was to come.

But nothing could have prepared them for this.

The villains didn't budge.

"Did you hear me?" the Monarch roared. "Attack Monstros City . . . rip it down . . . make them all pay for rejecting me!"

"No," Balthasar Bounder said, crossing his long hairy arms. "I don't think I'm up for it right now."

All his brothers followed suit, crossing their arms.

"I don't think they're up for it either," Balthasar informed the Monarch. "There's this little thing called loyalty that seems to be missing from this relationship."

"I feel so used," Bailey Bounder said, and began to cry on the shoulder of his brother Bernie.

The hooded figure clenched his fists in rage. "You call yourselves villains?" he cried. He turned his attention to the Gaseous Ghost and Vomitor.

"You will obey me," he demanded. "Go forth and make them all suffer for their actions!"

Vomitor shook his armored head. "Nope, don't think so. You're the one responsible for putting Vomitor in a bubble and making Vomitor float around in his own spew. No, thanks."

"He's got a point," the Ghost said. "Unless you're going to tell me that you didn't know anything about me getting sucked up in that vacuum cleaner of yours?"

"This is madness!" the Monarch screamed. "Do I have to do everything for myself?"

He again worked the controls on his giant remote. "Fine, be that way. I'll just destroy the city myself with weaponry of my own invention!"

The octocraft's limbs began to writhe in the air, and Billy was just about to call for his team when the mechanical octopus made a really sick-sounding noise.

"What's wrong with it?" the Monarch asked, turning to stare at the tentacled craft.

"Have you had your oil changed recently?" the slime-covered lackey asked.

"Maybe it needs a tune-up," said the red-skinned one.

The octocraft was smoldering, big clouds of thick, black smoke billowing from inside.

"How can this be?" the Monarch asked. "My octocraft is the ultimate example of microtechnology and robotics, the cutting edge of mechanical animals built to cause total destruction."

The craft moaned suddenly and dropped to the ground with a thunderous crash, all eight of its tentacles going completely limp.

"That thing's down for the count," Halifax said.

"Wonder what's wrong? It seemed perfectly fine and ready for mass destruction just a few minutes ago," Billy added.

Something scrambled out from inside the octocraft—two somethings, actually.

Ferdinand the dragon and Zis-Boom-Bah came running down the platform, their mouths filled with what looked like wires and gears from somewhere inside the mechanical octopus.

"I think we've got our answer," Billy said, watching

as the tiny beasties fled into the crowd, finally jumping up into Archebold's arms.

"There's my good boy and girl," the goblin squealed in baby talk, planting kisses atop their heads.

The two continued to chew their octocraft guts happily.

"We should probably think about getting out of here," the slimy lackey said, pulling his master's sleeve.

"Yeah, now might be a good time to think about gettin' you know, while the gettin' is good," said the other, eyeing the crowd.

The Monarch turned to flee the scene.

Billy thought about just letting the guy go. He'd obviously had a really bad day, what with his plans falling apart and then his octocraft breaking down. But then Billy thought better of it. This guy was dangerous and needed to be stopped before he could cause any more trouble.

"Stop right there!" Billy cried in his heroic voice.

The Monarch turned slightly, and glared at Billy from within his hood, but he didn't stop.

Billy jogged toward the fleeing Monarch and his lackeys. He passed the Bounder boys, who were still standing around with their arms crossed defiantly.

"Don't look at us," Balthasar said. "We aren't doing a thing."

The Monarch was crawling over a section of limp tentacles when Billy pounced.

The owl swooping in on his prey, he thought. He landed on his stomach just missing the monarch himself but managing to grab hold of his robe.

"Gotcha!" Billy announced.

The Monarch kept running, unaware that Billy was holding on tightly. There was a ripping sound. . . . And suddenly, the robe and hood were torn away to reveal at last the mysterious visage of the Monarch.

Billy couldn't believe his eyes.

The Monarch was an older man, dressed in the most unusual of outfits. He was wearing what could only have been described as an Owlboy costume.

The Monarch froze in his tracks, looking down at the costume as if seeing it for the very first time.

"I knew his voice sounded familiar!" Artemus cried, and he and his goblin friends came to stand alongside Billy.

"Who is he?" Billy asked.

"That's Preston Stickwell," the old goblin announced, pointing at the man. "The missing Owlboy!"

It was as if Billy had been zapped with the paralysis ray all over again. He couldn't believe it.

The missing Owlboy was the Monarch.

The missing Owlboy was a bad guy.

CHAPTER 10

It was even more disturbing than learning that Darth was Luke's dad, and that had been pretty darn disturbing.

An eerie silence had fallen over the street as everyone stared at the old man dressed in the Owlboy costume. It was as if somebody had turned the volume down to zero on the stereo of life.

Even Victoria was quiet.

Billy just didn't know how to react. This was Preston Stickwell, the Owlboy who had disappeared, making way for Billy's own eventual turn as the costumed hero of Monstros City. Nobody had had any idea what had happened to him, and to see him like this? It was a complete and total nightmare.

And it seemed as if Preston was experiencing a bit of the nightmare himself. The old man looked down at the costume he was wearing, his face wrinkling into a look of absolute horror.

"No," the old Owlboy said. "What have I done?"

Preston looked really upset, and as he gazed around, Billy thought that he actually looked surprised at what he was seeing. Almost as if he didn't remember being responsible for any of it.

"Let me talk to 'im," Artemus said, gripping Billy's arm and moving toward the man.

"Preston," the old goblin called out. "It's me . . . Artemus."

The former Owlboy's face went from pained to crazy. "Oh no," he yelled, his eyes bugging. "You're not getting away from me that easily."

Billy was startled by the sudden change in the man's emotions, which had gone from sad and sorry to angry and wild in a heartbeat. And then there was his voice.

Billy could have sworn that the sound of Preston's voice had changed, too.

The former Owlboy opened one of the pouches on his belt and removed what Billy recognized to be a smoke bomb.

"He's gonna make a run for it!" Billy cried as Preston

threw the bomb down, shattering the casing and filling the air with thick billowing smoke.

Preston spun around and dove into the smoke, moving pretty spryly for an old dude, Billy thought.

They couldn't let Preston get away. Billy knew, deep down in his gut, that there was a bigger mystery here . . . a humongoid mystery that needed to be solved. Adjusting his goggles, Billy went to infrared so that he could see the shape of Preston Stickwell's body heat as the old man and his monstrous lackeys attempted to flee.

"Not so fast, Owlboy," Billy warned, then turned to his right to find Morty. "Care to give me a hand with this, Morty?"

Billy grabbed hold of the wheelchair and wheeled it into the roiling smoke before the skeletal goblin could even answer.

And his aim couldn't have been better.

The goblin in the wheelchair seemed to zero in on Preston and his two lackeys like a guided missile, colliding with the back of the former Owlboy's legs and sending them all spinning into the air—a jumble of arms and legs, wheelchair parts, and bones.

Billy and the others charged through the gradually clearing smoke.

"Good job, Morty!" Artemus cheered as he and the other old goblins retrieved the bones of their friend.

Preston Stillwell lay on the ground, moaning from

his collision with Morty. His lackeys lay nearby in an unconscious heap.

"He's an Owlboy too?" Victoria asked, standing by Billy's side.

"Used to be," Billy said.

"I can't look at him," Archebold said, turning around and burying his face in Halifax's shoulder. "It just makes me too sad."

The troll patted his friend's shoulder and tried to console him. "There, there, pally. It'll be all right."

Billy hoped that what Halifax said was true, but he wasn't sure. The old goblins were just standing there, disappointment on their faces as they gazed down at the guy who had once been a hero to the city of monsters, but now was something else altogether.

Preston moaned again, his eyelids flickering as he slowly regained consciousness. He moved his head from side to side as if trying to rouse himself from a really bad dream.

"He don't look like a bad guy," Victoria said, squatting down beside the former Owlboy for a closer look.

Billy was about to tell her not to get too close, that Preston could still be considered a dangerous supervillain, when the little girl pointed something out.

"Ewwww," she squealed, wrinkling up her nose. "What's that sticking out of his ear?"

Billy moved a little closer. There *was* something

sticking out of the former Owlboy's ear. It almost looked like a tail!

"I don't know what that is," Billy said. He almost reached down to touch it, but thought better of it. "Does anybody have any tweezers?"

Halifax immediately went through the front pocket of his overalls, pulling all kinds of stuff from the seemingly bottomless pouch. Four salamis, a stepstool, three lit candles and a toolbox filled with tools all came out of the pocket before the tweezers.

"I thought I had a pair," the troll said, smiling and handing them to Billy.

Billy thanked his friend before turning back to Preston Stickwell, who seemed to be reviving.

"What do you think you're doing?" Preston demanded. Before the man could cause any more trouble, Billy squeezed the tweezers, and took hold of the segmented tail that stuck out from the old man's ear canal.

Preston screamed.

"Get away from there. . . . Leave me alone!"

There was real panic in the man's voice, and that only made Billy more eager to learn what he was pulling on.

Billy gave the tail another good tug. The end squirmed around, trying to escape and crawl back inside Preston's head.

It's like trying to pull a piece of spaghetti from a running vacuum cleaner hose, Billy thought, his tongue sticking out of a corner of his mouth as he concentrated. He squeezed the metal pincers tight and kept pulling as hard as he could.

"Is that his brain?" Victoria asked.

"Looks more like some kind of bug," Archebold said.

"A bug, you say?" the goblin's grandfather said with a sudden curiosity. He and his pals had just finished re-assembling Morty in his wheelchair, and now they turned their full attention to Billy.

"I think it's coming!" Billy said excitedly, being careful not to pull too hard. That was all he would need, to have a piece of the thing break off and leave the remainder of it to tunnel back inside Preston's head.

Artemus moved closer, squatting down beside Billy.

"Looks like a worm," the old goblin observed.

That was exactly what it was.

The worm came free of Preston's ear with a wet-sounding *pop!* and it immediately began to squeal.

Billy wasn't sure if he'd ever seen anything quite this disgusting. The worm had been *inside* the man's *head*.

"Can you say '*Ewwwwww!*'?" Billy said, holding the tweezers up so everybody could see what he'd caught.

"Son of a gun," Artemus barked, and the old-timers nodded in understanding.

"What's going on?" Billy asked.

"That's not just any old worm," the goblin said.

"That's the Brain Worm," Saul grumbled.

"One of Owlboy's most dangerous foes," Percy continued.

Morty coughed out a cloud of dust in solidarity with his brethren.

"The Brain Worm?" Billy questioned, holding the squirming worm closer to his face for a better look.

"Yes, the Brain Worm," the tiny creature suddenly said, startling Billy. "But it has been many years since somebody last called me by that name."

"It talks!" Billy squeaked in surprise.

"Of course I talk," the worm grumbled.

"And it can do much worse than that," Artemus explained. The old goblin took the tweezers from Billy.

"The Brain Worm was always at the top of our most-villainous list," he went on. "It has the ability to take over its victims by crawling inside their ears and living in their brain, using their bodies to commit its dastardly crimes."

The Brain Worm chuckled, dangling from the tweezers. "I did much more than commit crimes!" it explained. "I created a criminal empire. There wasn't an evildoer in Monstros that wasn't somehow working for me. I was the Monarch, and I ruled this place with an iron fist."

Artemus brought the evil worm closer to his face. "And you used our poor Owlboy to do it."

"That was my greatest achievement," the worm

chortled. "Once I was able to enter his ear, his body became mine."

"I'm disappointed in myself," the old goblin said, shaking his head. "I should have put two and two together; the Brain Worm was one of the villains Preston was hunting when he disappeared," Artemus said sadly. "Guess this shows what kind of a sidekick *I* was."

Percy put his arm around his friend, and Saul patted him on the back.

Victoria stood before the dangling Brain Worm, hands on her hips, looking it right in the eyes.

"Now, who would want to do something so mean?" Victoria asked it. "What did the old Owlboy ever do to you?"

"He had what I could never have," the Brain Worm answered.

"Arms and legs?" Victoria suggested.

"No," the Worm barked. "A city that loved him."

"Oh," Victoria said, nodding.

"I always wanted to be a hero, even as a larva, but everybody laughed at me. They said I was too small . . . too ugly . . ."

"Too wormy?" Victoria suggested.

She was all about helping.

"Yes, too wormy," the Brain Worm went on. "And I swore that I would have my revenge on all those who said that I could never be a superhero . . . that I would make them want me. I would show them what a fantastic hero I could be."

"But you were a bad guy?"

"For a time . . . I needed to show them how much they needed me . . . how this new Owlboy was a failure."

"Hey!" Billy cried. "I'm not a failure. I think I'm doing pretty good. Stopped you, didn't I?"

Victoria giggled. "Billy's a great big failure," she said, starting one of her crazy dances.

Billy had almost started to feel bad for the Brain Worm too.

Almost.

He turned around to see where the chief and his men were. They seemed to have things under control. Some of the officers were monitoring the crowds, while others were getting the Monarch's villains ready for their journey back to Beelzebub.

"Hey, Chief, I've got another one for you," Billy said, taking the tweezers from Artemus.

Bloodwart's rocky body stomped over to Billy and extended a hand that looked as though it had been carved from granite.

"With pleasure, Owlboy," Chief Bloodwart said, taking the tweezers from him. "Ugly little beastie, ain't he?"

"Why don't you put me a little bit closer to your ear and I'll show you how ugly I am," the Brain Worm suggested.

"I've got enough things inside my head right now," the chief answered, carrying the worm to a transport bus that had just pulled up to take the villains back to prison. "But I'm sure the nice folks over at Beelzebub will have a comfy cell in the shape of a skull that you can crawl up into."

Billy breathed a sigh of relief as he watched the worm get carried off; this had been the wildest adventure in Monstros yet. He turned back to his friends to see that Artemus and the other old goblins were helping Preston Stickwell up.

"Where am I?" the old man asked, looking around. "I'm still in Monstros City, right?"

"That you are," Artemus said. "You've been away for a little while, but now you're back."

Preston slowly brought a hand to his chin. "No," he said. "I haven't been away. . . . I've been here all along . . . and I've done some horrible things!" His face crumpled.

Billy couldn't stand to see the old man look so sad.

"It wasn't you, sir," Billy said. "It was the Brain Worm. The Brain Worm did these things, not you."

The former hero looked down at Billy, surprised. "You're . . . you're Owlboy too?" he asked.

"Yes sir," Billy said. "I took over after you'd been gone for quite some time."

"And he's doing a bang-up job, I might add," Artemus said.

Halifax and Archebold beamed proudly.

"It was nothing, really," Archebold said. "I just needed to whip him into shape."

"I think he's gonna work out fine," Halifax added.

Walter the firefly stuck his head out from Archebold's pocket.

"And I agree," the bug said.

Billy didn't believe it—even Walter thought he was doing a good job?

Preston removed one of his gloves and touched his own face. "I've been gone for a very long time," the older man said, the tips of his fingers tracing his wrinkles. "I'm glad they found somebody to take my place." He smiled. "Somebody to protect the city that I love."

And then Billy had the most terrible thought: the only reason he'd been recruited as the new Owlboy was that Preston had gone missing, and now that the original Owlboy had returned . . .

Preston extended his hand to Billy.

"Thank you," the old Owlboy said as the two shook hands.

"I guess you're gonna want your job back, right?" Billy asked, doing everything he could to keep his voice from cracking with disappointment.

Preston managed a small, sad smile.

"Oh, no," the old man said with a shake of his head. "I'm too old for this kind of work. From what my friends say, you're doing a most excellent job, and I have a lot of catching up to do. Being evil really cramped my style."

Billy felt an enormous weight lifted from his shoulders. He didn't know what he would have done if he couldn't be Owlboy anymore.

"See, Billy," Victoria said. "You're not a great big failure after all." She giggled evilly, and again Billy wondered if the small child might be possessed by the devil.

"Thanks, Destructo *Lass*," he said.

"I am not Destructo *Lass*," she said with an angry scowl. "I'm Destructo—"

"What's that, Destructo Lass?" he asked, cutting her off and putting a hand to his ear. "I couldn't hear you, Destructo Lass."

She looked as though she just might blow a gasket. Billy was about to apologize, tell her to calm down and maybe promise to play grocery store when they got back to Bradbury, when she raised one of her legs, preparing to bring it down in a stomp that could send devastating tremors through downtown Monstros.

"Don't stomp your foot and I'll buy you that fairy princess tiara that's in the window of the Hero's Hovel!"

The words seemed to just spill from Billy's mouth, surprising him. The fairy princess tiara had accidentally been sent to the Hovel in an order of action figures, and Cole had never gotten around to sending it back. Eventually, he'd stuck it in the window, hoping that a sucker would come along someday and buy it.

Victoria had seen it not too long ago and had been bugging Billy about it since.

"You will?" she asked with a smile, balancing on one foot.

Billy couldn't believe it, but knew that this was a simple way to avoid a big-time problem. "Only if you don't use your Destructo powers and stamp your foot," he said.

"You got yourself a deal, bro!" she squealed happily.

As she gently brought her sneakered foot down to the street, a powerful tremor that Billy felt in his teeth shook the street to its very bedrock.

"I didn't do it!" Victoria yelled, throwing her hands on her head.

The ground shook again violently. Billy watched as a section of street bulged upward, the pavement splitting open as something huge and monstrous emerged.

It was just one of those nights.

Mother Sassafras looked very angry.

The giant troll woman pulled her body up through

202

the hole she had torn in the city street from the sewer tunnels below.

"Oh man, I thought we took care of her," Billy said, stumbling back from the awful sight of the Sassafras Siblings' mother.

"Me too," Archebold squeaked. "Guess they weren't as down for the count as we thought they were."

She crawled up onto the street on her hands and knees, her face and flower-print dress stained with a variety of foulness from the Monstros City sewer system. Her hair looked like the head of a mop that had been used to clean up an oil spill.

"Where are they?" the troll mother bellowed, climbing to her feet and wobbling on tree-trunk-thick legs. "Where are the monsters that did this to me?"

Sigmund and Sireena emerged behind their mother, covered in sewer scum and carrying their massively destructive weapons.

"Here's your gun, Mother," Sigmund said, handing his mother a pistol dripping with sludge.

Her ugly face wrinkled in disgust as she took the weapon from her son.

"Is this what I have been reduced to?" she screamed again. "Using weapons covered in filth?" She stared at the gun and the thick stream that slowly oozed from the barrel.

"This is all because of you," she scolded, her beady eyes scrutinizing the heroes standing before her. "You couldn't leave well enough alone. Monstros was doing perfectly fine without an Owlboy, but you had to come along and foul everything up for my poor children."

Sireena and Sigmund now stood on either side of their monstrous parent.

"All we wanted was to be king and queen of Monstros," Sireena roared. "But no, Mr. 'I'm Owlboy and I have to protect the innocent from harm' has to come along and spoil everything my brother and I worked so hard for."

"All we wanted was to strike terror in the hearts of the citizens of Monstros. Is that too much to ask?" Sigmund demanded, his voice cracking with emotion.

"There, there, my sweets," Mother Sassafras said, patting her son's and daughter's backs. "Mother will make certain that all your dreams come true. It's what a good mommy does for her children."

The Sassafrases opened fire, their energy weapons blowing away huge chunks of street and building as Billy and the other heroes tried to duck for cover.

"I'm tired of being Destructo Ballerina," Victoria complained.

Halifax had scooped the child up and was running in a zigzag as Sireena tried to blow them away.

The streets were again in total panic. Citizens ran

around screaming at the tops of their lungs. Peeking out over the top of the car he'd jumped behind for cover, Billy saw that his team was trapped, pinned down by the Sassafrases' rapid gunfire.

They needed a distraction if they were ever going to reach the villainous family and take them out.

Billy gulped, ready to do something that might be considered very dumb, but he didn't see a choice. He was the leader of this team, and he had to lead by example.

He got ready to jump up from his cover, hoping that somebody would have the good sense to take the Sassafrases down while he was risking his life.

He really would hate getting killed for nothing.

"No, let me," said a voice.

Billy turned to see Preston Stickwell standing beside him.

He started to object, but the former Owlboy silenced him with a gesture.

"I've got some things to make up for," the older man said, and with a smile stepped out from behind the car and into the Sassafrases' line of sight.

"Oh, look, an old bird," Sireena cackled.

"Two Owlboys in one day," Sigmund said, amused. "Monstros will be afraid of us forever."

"Enough with the chatter, you two," Mother Sassafras said.

And just as she was about to fire, the old Owlboy produced something from one of his pouches and aimed it at the trigger-happy threesome. A beam of yellow light pulsed from the device, striking Mother Sassafras first, then spreading to the others.

All three suddenly drifted up from the ground, the victims of a sudden loss of gravity.

"This again?" Sireena complained, trying to keep from twirling around.

"I thought this was a Monarch trick," Sigmund said as he tumbled through the air.

"Doesn't mean the technology can't be put to good use," the former Owlboy said, watching the trolls float above the city street.

"Put us down this instant!" Mother Sassafras commanded.

"Or you'll what?" Preston asked with a chuckle. "You're in no position to make demands."

Mother Sassafras became enraged, shoving her pistol down the front of her dress as she reached out to snatch her daughter's bigger, and nastier, rifle.

"Mister Shooty!" Sireena cried as she was relieved of her favorite weapon.

"You were warned," Mother Sassafras said with a snarl as she fired Mister Shooty at the former Owlboy.

The recoil of the weapon threw the weightless troll backward into her daughter, sending them both cannonballing through the air toward one of Monstros's taller buildings. They hit the building with the force of a wrecking ball, punching a huge hole in the side.

Villains are as dumb as a bag of rocks, the comic book Owlboy had said in the second issue of his monthly comic, and Billy had to agree.

Sigmund did the only thing that made sense to his pea-sized brain: he fired his weapon too. . . .

And launched himself into orbit. Well, maybe not into orbit, but high enough that those on the ground lost sight of the Sassafras sibling.

"Well, that takes care of that," Preston said with a smile, handing the antigravity weapon to Billy. "You can have this if you like."

"Thanks," Billy said as he took the device, certain that it would come in handy in his war against evil.

"Let me have that," Victoria said, attempting to take the antigrav weapon from his hand. "I want to float like a balloon too."

Billy looked down at the five-year-old and considered the image of her floating off into space, never to bother him again. The prospect brought an evil smile to his face.

"No way," he said, pushing her away and hiding the device in one of the pouches on his utility belt. "I can only imagine the trouble you'd cause with it."

She looked as though she was about to have another

tantrum, so Billy used his secret weapon again. "There's a certain fairy princess tiara that's gonna stay in the window of a certain store if a certain somebody isn't good," he warned.

Victoria crossed her arms and scowled.

The citizens of Monstros were emerging from their hiding places. Billy noticed Sammy over by his store, waving to him.

"We should probably give Sammy a hand and then think about getting back to the Roost," Billy said as he waved back.

Halifax and Archebold were looking over the octo-craft.

"How are we gonna get this back to the Roost?" Halifax asked, stroking his hairy chin in thought.

"I always wanted my very own robotic octopus," Archebold said, clapping his hands together gleefully.

The sound of screeching tires and brakes alerted Billy to another potential danger. "What now?" he said, exasperatedly throwing his hands up into the air.

A long black limousine was making its way down Mortis Street, its horn beeping for citizens to get out of the way.

"Who the heck could this be?" Artemus asked.

Billy shook his head. He didn't have a clue.

The back door of the vehicle opened and the mayor

of Monstros scrambled out, his rat face twitching excitedly.

"Oh no," Billy heard Halifax say behind him. "I better hide or he's gonna yell at me some more for filling his house with vomit."

The mayor slammed the door closed and smiled. . . . At least, Billy thought it was a smile. It was hard to tell with rats.

"There's my favorite superhero," the mayor said, clasping his hands.

"Favorite hero?" Billy asked. "Didn't sound like that on the news the other night."

"Oh, that?" the mayor said dismissively. "They took me completely out of context." He threw his arm around Billy's shoulders.

Photographers and cameramen from the various newspapers and television news channels scrambled around them as the mayor smiled happily.

"We're a great team, aren't we, Owlboy?" the mayor said, his long rat teeth protruding over his thin lips as he beamed for the cameras.

"Y'think?" Billy asked.

"Oh brother," Artemus said as he tossed his head back. "This guy is shoveling it on pretty darn thick. He wouldn't happen to be running for reelection any time soon, would he?"

Victoria jumped in front of them.

"I want to be in the picture," she said, waving at the television cameras.

"Go away!" the mayor barked, trying to shoo her away with his furry, rat hands.

"No, she stays," Billy said, staring into the rat's beady eyes.

The mayor looked as if he was about to get angry, but Billy stared really, really hard.

"In fact, I want all of my team in the pictures," he demanded.

As the mayor seemed to realize that he wasn't going to win this one, his ratty face broke into an enormous smile. "Of course! The more the merrier," he agreed with an uncomfortable chuckle, gesturing for them all to get into the picture.

And they all took their positions; Archebold, Halifax and Victoria on one side: Preston Stickwell, Artemus, Saul, Percy and Morty on the other.

"Great shot," said the photographer, whose head was one giant eyeball, as he aimed his camera. "This is gonna be prime front-page material."

Billy smiled mightily as the bulb's flash caused tiny fireworks displays to dance in front of his eyes.

"Is that really gonna be on the front page?" Billy asked the eyeball.

"Most likely," he answered.

"Well, I've got the perfect headline if you're interested," Billy said.

The eyeball set his camera down on the ground and took a notebook from one of his pants pockets. "All right, let's have it."

"Heroes send supervillains packing," Billy said with a grin. "Monstros City under the protection of new superhero team."

The eyeball smiled as he wrote. "That's good," he said, reading the headline back. "Does this new team have a name?"

"The Flock of Fury," Billy announced, his voice loud and clear so that all assembled on the downtown street could hear. "We're the Flock of Fury!"

CHAPTER 11

Due to the strange way that time passed in Monstros City, it was still late Friday night when Billy and Victoria crawled out of the crypt in the Sprylock Family mausoleum.

Billy was actually glad to be back. This last adventure to Monstros had been exhausting.

Victoria waited impatiently for him to change out of his Owlboy costume. The little girl had already been wearing her Destructo Ballerina costume when they'd first hooked up, so there was no need for her to change.

"C'mon, Billy," she said, stamping her foot—but not causing any devastating effects. "I don't got all night. I'm 'zausted."

"Yeah, yeah, yeah," he said, pulling on the hooded sweatshirt he'd taken from the rolling suitcase he'd originally brought to Monstros.

Finished dressing, he poked his head out from the burial chamber to be sure that nobody was watching. The cemetery was eerily quiet.

"All clear," Billy said, pushing the door open so that they could exit.

They walked the path in the cold night air, Billy pulling his suitcase loaded with his science fair projects/Monstros City secret weapons behind him.

The effort suddenly reminded him of what he had to do on Saturday, and he found himself becoming depressed. He had an entire day ahead of him during which he'd be doing a science fair project all by himself.

He helped Victoria over the stone wall into his yard, then tossed the suitcase over before climbing it himself.

"What're you gonna do tomorrow, Billy?" Victoria asked him as they crossed his yard.

"Got some stuff to do for school," he told her sadly.

"I think I'm gonna be a fairy princess tomorrow," she said after some thought. "Gonna need a special tiara if I'm gonna be a real fairy princess."

She stopped and stared at him with eager eyes.

"I know, I know," he said. "I promised I'd buy you the fairy princess tiara at the Hero's Hovel."

He almost considered blowing off the science fair work, throwing his hands in the air and screaming, "Who cares!" Then on Saturday he would get up late, have some breakfast and maybe play a few video games before heading off to the Hovel to peruse some comic books and pick up the tiara he'd promised to buy Victoria. *Why should I be the only one that gives a rat's behind about this stupid project?* he asked himself.

"Hey," Victoria interrupted. "What about my fairy tiara?"

Billy was about to say that he'd go get it for her tomorrow, but realized, sadly, that if he were to do that, he'd likely feel guilty about it all day, and he'd just end up not having a good time because he'd be thinking about all the crap he wasn't doing.

"I'll get it for you during the week," he said morosely.

"You promise?" the little girl asked.

Billy crossed his chest. "Cross my heart and hope to die."

She studied his face, looking for a sign that he was lying. Finding none, she went on her way.

"Okey-doke," Victoria said, walking across the yard and squeezing through some bushes to go into her own yard. "See ya later, Billy."

A second later she was back. Victoria stood beside a bush, watching Billy with a smile on her cute—yet strangely disturbing—face.

"What now?" he asked, his patience on the wane.

"Next time we go back to Monstros I'm gonna be Destructo Fairy Princess," she said, eyes twinkling.

"Awesome," he said, making a mental note to do everything in his power to make sure that day never came.

And then she was gone again, running up the steps of her back porch and sneaking into the house.

Billy opened the garage door, went inside and set his suitcase in the far corner. He walked over to the other corner of the garage to see if the uncharted passage to the shadow paths was still there, but it had obviously closed. Archebold had said something about the instability of those particular kinds of paths and how they often closed without any real reason. Billy had sort of hoped he would find the passage still open, providing him with another opportunity to escape what he still needed to do.

But deep down he knew: even if it had been open, he wouldn't have gone through it.

He felt himself growing angry—angry at all the work he had to do, and angry at himself for being the only one doing it.

But what choice is there? a wimpy voice whined inside his head.

He'd always hated that voice, but he knew that it was often right. There wasn't a choice, really; he needed to do the work so the project would get done.

Briefly he thought about the alternative.

If he didn't do the project, they'd all fail science for sure, and he'd end up suffering just as much as his stupid enemies.

It was so frustrating he wanted to scream. It was the same kind of frustration he'd felt when he'd realized that he needed to do something to save Monstros, even though it had seemed as though they no longer wanted or needed him.

And how had he reacted? He'd put together a team.

Billy felt the gears slowly begin to turn inside his head.

I put together a team, he reminded himself. *I acted like a leader and put together a team to solve a problem.*

And suddenly he felt as though he could do that again. Yeah, it would probably all blow up in his face and end up with him receiving atomic wedgies for the rest of his life, but he realized that it needed to be done.

He wasn't going to do this science fair project alone.

Billy was going to lead his team, atomic wedgies for life or not.

On the way to Randy Kulkowski's house the next morning, Billy wondered if during his last trip to Monstros he had maybe lost his mind.

How else could he explain it?

He wondered if maybe the Gaseous Ghost's noxious fumes had somehow affected his brain, turning him into a total nutjob, or at least very, very stupid.

Billy knew how absolutely crazy this was, walking right into the lion's den—heck, into the lion's freakin' mouth—but it didn't stop him. He kept right on going, all the while practicing exactly what he was going to say to the boy.

If anybody had heard him, they would have definitely called Happydale State Hospital for the Looney, but it was still relatively early and the streets of Bradbury were peacefully quiet.

Maybe I can catch him when he's practically still asleep, Billy thought, checking the numbers on the houses as he walked. *That way he'll think it was all a dream and not tear me limb from limb when he finally catches up to me.*

Nope, that wouldn't do any good, he corrected himself. If he was going to do this, he was going to do this right, despite the threat of bodily harm.

Billy had decided that he was just going to tell it like it was. He would explain that he had no problem contributing to the science project, but he wasn't going to do the whole thing without any help.

He could already feel the burning sting of the first atomic wedgie.

But it didn't stop him.

Realizing that he'd walked too far down Cottage

Street, he stopped and retraced his steps until he found the house he'd been searching for.

The mailboxes out front told him that the Kulkowskis lived on the first floor, and before he could even think about getting the heck out of there, he was climbing the stairs and pushing the doorbell.

All the things he had practiced—all the things that he was going to say to Randy—flowed through his mind in a tidal wave.

He was about to push the buzzer again when the door suddenly opened.

A large woman in a flowery housecoat stood in the doorway looking at him. For a moment, he thought Mother Sassafras had somehow escaped Beelzebub prison and relocated to Cottage Street in Bradbury, Massachusetts.

"Yeah?" she asked, painted fingernails scratching her pronounced belly.

"Is Randy home?" Billy asked, not believing that he was actually asking such a thing. It wouldn't have sounded any crazier if he'd asked to be infected with the bubonic plague.

She looked at him for what seemed like hours but was likely only seconds, then stepped back and to the side so that he could see into the house and down the hall to the kitchen.

"Randy, you got a visitor," she said, disappearing through a doorway on the left and leaving Billy with a good view of the kitchen at the end of the hall.

Billy could see him there, sitting at the table, turkey leg halfway to his mouth.

A *turkey leg?* the wimpy voice screamed in his ear, finding something else to complain about. *Who eats a turkey leg for breakfast?*

"Hooten," Randy croaked, and before another word could come out of his caveman face, Billy opened up the floodgates and let him have it.

"I know that you'll probably kill me for saying this, but you and the others are gonna help me with the science fair project whether you want to or not it's not just me getting a grade on this it's all of us and I'm not about to do all the work even if you threaten to give me atomic wedgies for the rest of my life and if you think . . ."

Billy couldn't have stopped himself if he'd tried; it all came spilling out, sentence after sentence.

"And it was my idea, and I'm willing to let all you guys have a piece but I'm not going to do all the work. I'm not. I'm not. I'm not. I'll do some of the work, like you'll do some of the work, and Mitchell will do some of the work, and Penny will do some of the work and Darious will give us all the creeps, but he'll do some of the work and . . ."

Randy looked like he was paralyzed, his eyes getting wider and wider the more Billy talked at him.

And finally, when it had all come out, Billy just stopped talking, turned around, and headed for home.

Billy had to admit, it had felt pretty good telling Randy off like that.

After closing the refrigerator door, he brought the milk over to the kitchen table and poured some on his cereal.

This could very well be my last meal of Sugar-Crusted Bombers, he thought, watching the cereal in his bowl start to swell up with milk. He pulled out a kitchen chair and sat down.

He'd already gone upstairs and fished through his collection to find a few of his absolute favorite comics. If this was to be his last breakfast, he wanted to be sure he was doing something awesome while eating it.

He picked up his favorite spoon—Billy had no idea why this was his favorite, it was just the spoon that he used every day—and plunged it into the bowl, picking up one of the pieces. "You are a gorgeous thing," he said to the saturated chocolate ball, anticipating every aspect of his first mouthful: the cold milk, the squishy feeling of the spongy breakfast bite on his tongue, the spurt of milk miraculously turning to chocolatey syrup as he chewed.

Heaven.

And after the first bite, the very first issue of Owlboy.

He set his spoon down, carefully removed the fragile comic book from the bag and laid it on the table—making sure there wasn't anything wet or sticky there first, of course.

This was it, the original Owlboy comic book adventure, and the beginning of so much more.

Billy closed his eyes, letting the smell of the old comic book waft up into his nose, mixing with the chocolate taste and smell of his cereal. *Why can't the world smell like this all the time?*

So he ate his cereal—two bowls, actually—and read his comics, thinking about how sad it would be when he was dead.

He guessed his death would likely come sometime at school on Monday. Billy made a mental note to say goodbye to all his pals when he first got in, because who knew how long he would last? He doubted he would make it to lunchtime.

Deciding then that he would play a game of Galactic Rangers, and finally destroy the Antarian Death Fleet as it prepared to release its zombie larvae upon the city of Shineopolis, he took his empty bowl to the sink. He was getting ready to slip his comics back into their plastic bags so that he could return them to his collection when there was a pounding on the back door.

Billy's heart leapt in his chest.

Had death come for him here . . . in his own home?

He stared at the door, wishing that he had some kind of laser vision, imaging twin beams of red energy blasting through the door and turning whatever it was outside to screaming dust.

But what if it's only the paperboy? That wouldn't be good.

The pounding came again and he knew.

The paperboy didn't knock like that: only Death in the apelike form of Randy Kulkowski knocked like that.

Billy was tempted to run down the hall and up the stairs to his parents' room, not to beg for their help but to tell them how much he loved them and how he wished that he had seen the day that they finally raised his allowance to fifteen bucks a month instead of a measly twelve.

Again came the knock; more insistent, more violent.

Death wanted him bad.

Slowly, Billy crept toward the kitchen door and peeked behind the curtain over the window to see if he was mistaken.

He wasn't; Randy Kulkowski's apelike face glared at him through the window as he waited on the porch for Billy to answer.

"Hey, Hooten, open up," Death commanded.

Not opening the door wasn't an option. Billy knew the kind of beast Randy was, knew that he would stand and knock all day if he had to, which would just wake up Mom and Dad, making them mad enough to open the door and feed Billy to the hungry Kulkowski beast.

It was time to face the music.

As he unlocked the door, turning the knob to pull it open, he still had to admit: it had felt really good telling Randy how he thought it should be.

And that was a feeling that he would take with him to his early grave, or at least the intensive care unit at Bradbury Hospital.

"About freakin' time," Randy snarled, his hands shoved in the pockets of his stained winter jacket. "Are we just gonna stand out here all day or are we gonna work on that science project?"

It took a minute for Billy to process the information.

Randy Kulkowski was not alone. Standing at the foot of his back porch were Mitchell Spivey, Darious Fontague and Penny Feryurthotuss.

At first glance, Billy believed that Death had brought a team to dispose of him, that they were all going to take turns killing him slowly for defying them, but then he heard Randy's words replay inside his head.

Are we gonna stand out here all day or are we gonna work on that science project?

"Excuse me?" Billy squeaked.

Randy smiled, showing off uneven, crusty teeth. "Bet you think yer hearing things," he said. He looked down to the others and they were laughing and smiling as well.

"Bet he thinks he's hearing things," Mitchell repeated, cackling like a maniac.

"Thought you was gonna have some kind of nervous breakdown or something at my house," Randy explained. "Didn't want to get blamed for it, so I thought we should probably help you out with the project so you didn't bust a blood vessel or anything." He looked to the gang. "Right?"

They nodded, none of them looking all that thrilled but at the same time not wanting to incur the wrath of the Kulkowski monster.

"Hey, Billy, we're cool now about that Jell-O," Darious said with a flip of his head. "It's all water under the bridge."

"But I never took your Jell-O," Billy started to explain again, but gave up. "So let me get this straight," he said. "You guys have actually come to work on our science project . . . as a team." He waited, sure that there had to be some sort of punch line to all this.

Randy shrugged. "That looks to be the case," he said.

"So are we gonna do this or what?" Penny asked

with a whiplike snap of her gum. "I really hate science and stuff and would, y'know, like get this over with as soon as I can."

It's like being back in Monstros, Billy thought as he ducked back into the kitchen to grab his coat. The impossible was happening, but it was here this time, at his house in Bradbury, Massachusetts.

He had formed a team back in the city of monsters to handle something too big to handle on his own, and the same thing was about to happen here.

Amazing.

"Didn't think you had it in ya, Hooten," Randy said as they descended the steps from his porch and headed to the garage.

"You'd be surprised at what I can do, Randy," Billy said, opening the door on his workshop, where they would hopefully accomplish the task of creating the best science project imaginable. "Really, really surprised."

EPILOGUE

A few days later . . .

Using his key, Billy let himself into the lower level of the Roost from the shadow passages.

"Hello?" he called, pulling the key from the door and slipping it back into one of the pouches on his utility belt. "It's me."

"We're in here," Archebold answered.

Billy strolled into the chamber and over to the monitor station.

Archebold and Halifax were reclined in chairs in front of the multiple television screens broadcasting the various happenings all across Monstros City.

"What's up?" Billy asked, tugging on the ends of his

Owlboy gloves for a tighter fit. He was ready for some serious action tonight and had hoped that something big was brewing, but seeing his two friends now, he wasn't sure he'd be so lucky.

"Nothin'," Archebold said, eating what looked like fried beetles from a bag in his lap as he stared ahead at the screens.

"Yeah, nothing," Halifax reiterated, taking a sip from a mug that looked as if it had been made from a monkey skull.

There was a sudden screech and Billy turned to see Zis-Boom-Bah and Ferdinand waddling into the room.

"Hey, guys," Billy said, noticing that the dragon was carrying what appeared to be a rag, and Zis-Boom-Bah a spray bottle.

"What're you two up to?" he asked them.

They walked over to the monitor screens and began to clean them. Zis-Boom-Bah sprayed them first, and then Ferdinand wiped them with her cloth.

"Nice to see that at least two of you are keeping busy," Billy said, looking at Archebold and Halifax out of the corner of his eye.

"Since you took down the Monarch it's been really slow around here," Archebold said, having some more beetles.

"Yeah," Halifax agreed, staring with zombie eyes at

the monitors. "Almost like you proved how tough you are. Nobody wants to mess with you now."

"Hurmmm," Billy said, pulling up a footstool to sit down.

He started to watch the monitors as well. Monstros City appeared to be doing just fine, not a thing out of whack.

They sat there in silence for a while, Ferdinand and Zis-Boom-Bah continuing with their chore of cleaning the monitor screens. After the bottom row of screens had been cleaned, Ferdinand picked up Zis-Boom-Bah by the shoulders with her back feet, flying him up to the dusty television screens he could not reach.

"Hey, how was your science fair?" Archebold asked with as much enthusiasm as a three-toed sloth with sleeping sickness.

Billy shrugged but then smiled, remembering the day and what had transpired.

"Our model of Pompeii was a big hit," Billy said with a nod. "That is, until Randy activated the eruption of our model Vesuvius."

"Didn't work?" Halifax asked, sipping from his monkey skull.

"Oh, it worked," Billy explained. "It worked too good. I think Randy might have read my notes wrong about how much liquid detergent, vinegar and baking soda to put in."

"Sounds deadly," Archebold said, picking a piece of beetle out from between his teeth with the nail of his little finger.

"Not deadly . . . messy," Billy said with a laugh. "Fake lava covering everything and everybody. It was sort of like the real eruption of Vesuvius, only without the dying in agony part."

"Sorry it didn't go so great," Archebold said, examining the piece of whatever it was that he had unwedged from between his teeth.

"Sorry for what?" Billy asked. "We came in second place. Probably would have come in first if the kids were voting . . . they loved it. The adults, well, they had some issues with staining."

"Rub a little chupacabra blood on any stain and it'll come right out," Halifax said, looking away from the monitors momentarily. "It's true, I swear."

"Good to know," Billy said.

His eyes wandered to a particular screen that had just been cleaned by Zis-Boom-Bah and Ferdinand. It showed the Groaning Acres and some of the residents sitting out on the front porch.

"Hey, look at that," Billy said, pointing the screen out. "It's Artemus, Saul, Percy and Morty," he said, and then noticed that there was a human sitting among them.

"Is that Preston?" he asked.

"Yep," Archebold said. "He's living with my grandfather and his gang at Groaning Acres," the young goblin answered. "Seems to be getting along just fine and catching up on all the stuff he missed while he was evil."

"He's really good at line dancing," Halifax pointed out.

"That's great," Billy said, watching as the former Owlboy set up a checkers game for himself and Artemus.

Billy continued to watch the monitors, looking for a sign of something that was amiss, but everything was perfectly fine.

Boringly, perfectly fine.

Billy must've stared at those television screens for hours before he finally decided he couldn't stand it anymore. Usually Monstros was the most exciting place he could imagine, but tonight . . . being at home rearranging his underwear drawer would have been more exciting.

"All right, I've had just about enough of this," Billy said, standing up and stretching his arms above his head. His back popped loudly. "Think I'm gonna call it a night."

Archebold and Halifax barely responded.

"Take it easy, Billy," Archebold said. Ferdinand was

now lying in his lap, and the goblin was gently stroking the tiny dragon's head.

Halifax had fallen asleep and was snoring. Zis-Boom-Bah had crawled up onto his chest and was pulling things from the front pocket of the troll's overalls. The little monster had found half a donut and was now chomping on it eagerly.

"Maybe things will be more exciting tomorrow night," Billy said, tiredly shuffling from the room.

"Who knows," Archebold called after him. "This just might be how it is from now on. You might've done it, Billy. You might've finally driven evil from Monstros City."

Billy turned to respond to the comment when the air became filled with a familiar sound.

"Hoot! Hoot! Hoot! Hoot! Hoot! Hoot! Hoot!"

It was the danger alarm.

Archebold leapt from the chair, Ferdinand taking flight with a ruffle of her leathery wings.

"What is it?" Billy asked, his heartbeat quickening.

Halifax woke with a snort, screaming out loud as he saw all the things Zis-Boom-Bah had taken from his front pocket.

"I'm not sure," Archebold said, eyeing the various monitors, searching for a sign of danger.

"There!" the goblin exclaimed, pointing to a screen

that showed an aerial view of all of Monstros. Odd clouds were roiling in the sky above the city, lights flashing within their cottony mass.

"What do you think?" Billy said, going to stand beside his friend.

Flying saucers emerged from the thick cloud cover, and thousands of gray metal spaceships started to descend upon the city of monsters.

"I think the city is in big trouble," the goblin said, looking at Billy.

He couldn't help smiling at the potential danger.

"I wouldn't want it any other way," he said. "To the Owlmobile!"

THOMAS E. SNIEGOSKI is a novelist and comic book scripter who has worked for every major company in the comics industry.

He is also the author of the groundbreaking quartet of teen fantasy novels titled The Fallen, the first of which (*Fallen*) was produced as a television movie for the ABC Family Channel. He is also the author of *Force Majeure* and Sleeper Conspiracy, a new series published by Razorbill, and he has completed the first novel, *A Kiss Before the Apocalypse*, in a new supernatural mystery series. His other novels include *Buffy the Vampire Slayer/Angel: Monster Island* and *Angel: The Soul Trade*, each based on a popular television series. With Christopher Golden, he is the coauthor of the dark fantasy series The Menagerie, as well as the young readers' fantasy series OutCast, recently optioned by Universal Pictures.

Sniegoski was born and raised in Massachusetts, where he still lives with his wife, LeeAnne, and their Labrador retriever, Mulder. Please visit the author at www.sniegoski.com.

ERIC POWELL is the writer and artist of the award-winning comic book series The Goon, from Dark Horse Comics. He has also contributed work to such comic titles as *Arkham Asylum*, *Buffy the Vampire Slayer*, *Hellboy: Weird Tales*, *Star Wars Tales*, *The Incredible Hulk*, *MAD Magazine*, *Swamp Thing*, and *The Simpsons*.